The Best of CaféLit 11

The Best of CaféLit 11

an anthology

Edited by:
Liz Cox
Linda Flynn
Gill James
Madeleine McDonald
Hannah Retallick
Allison Symes

Chapeltown Books

British Library Cataloguing in Publication Data

A Record of this Publication is available from the British Library

ISBN 978-1-910542-89-7

This edition published 2022 by Chapeltown Books
Manchester, England

Contents

Foreword

This year we asked our editors to select their favourite stories in a particular month. Each editor has made a short introduction to the stories they have selected. We've aimed for a balance of shorter and longer stories, and of amusing and thought-provoking stories.

We hope you will enjoy them as much as we did.

JANUARY

It was a difficult job choosing the best 3,000 words or so that we published in January 2021. There are many other stories apart from the ones featured here that I would have liked to publish. Hopefully they might find their way into one of our single author collections or their authors might even decide to self-publish.

The choice of drink is spot on for Sharon Overend's Torn. *There is something as bitter and as refreshing as bitter lemon about this story.*

There is nostalgia and sadness in Alyson Faye's Two Brothers *as mother and daughter look at photos of brothers, uncle and father. The scent of the old lady's talcum powder evoke a childhood memory for the daughter.*

Allison Symes' flash fiction Flying Too High ***contrasts*** *with these two where in just a few words we find out how an aviator learns of his mistake.*

About the editor

Gill James, writer, editor, creative writing lecturer.

www.gilljameswriter.com/

Torn

Sharon Overend

Bitter lemon

I snap to attention as my teenage daughter charges toward me, a pair of garden shears clutched in her hand. Head spinning tantrums are nothing new in our household, but the introduction of sharp objects is new.

Blood rushes from my limbs and my hands tingle like when I wake from a nightmare. I'm on my knees. Two bags of black soil and a bouquet of four potted chrysanthemums crowd the flagstone walkway. I've just finished raking the first of the autumn leaves and pulled out the last of the summer flowers.

Her charge stops inches from me, her weapon held waist high, parallel to my face. She's breathing hard, her chest rises and falls in quick spastic jerks. Her cheeks are blotchy and tear-stained, her eyes wild.

"What's wrong, Cassie?" I ask. My left hand grips the side of the empty planter, my right hand curls around the handle of a semi-submerged trowel. I'm surprised not only because of the shears, but also that her face is tear-stained. She doesn't like to cry. Even when she was little and fell, her chin would quiver and her Adam's apple piston up and down as she fought to swallow back tears. I'm a crier and nothing drives her crazier than when my voice chokes.

"I want my phone back. If I don't call them, my friends will dump me." The autumn air is cool, but she's wearing shorts. Her leg muscles are tight, and like a horse in the starting gate, she shifts her weight from side-to-side.

"Your friends aren't going to dump you," I say and bring one hand to my forehead to shield my eyes from the glint bouncing off the blades. A halo of yellow surrounds her head.

Her eyes narrow and the shears follow my movements. "How would you know?" she asks. Her right eye turns in, the way it does when she's tired or manic. The scents of her lavender shampoo and a freshly turned garden hang in the open air between us. "You don't know anything about me, or my life."

I stare at her in disbelief. I know this child, my dramatic child, my middle child, the one we planned, the one who hadn't been an oops. I know each of my daughters. My eldest is quiet, studious, a deep thinker. The youngest is an athlete, the golden girl. And this child, the one wielding garden shears, the one always on the verge of hysterics, is the difficult one.

I leave the trowel upright in the dirt and push up from the ground.

"Put the shears down," I say. She's three inches taller than me, and I'm forced to look up into her face.

The tantrums began in her first months of life when colic robbed her of the comfort suckling at my breasts should have provided. Maybe her baby mind had concluded it was my milk, my breasts, her mommy, that made her belly cramp.

"I bet you wish I would."

Brat. Drama queen. Manipulator. Mental. Wounded. Words others have used to describe her, words I've used to grab her attention, needles pushed through a pincushion.

My fingers coil into a fist. Loose, dirt-encrusted garden gloves fold and bunch inside my palms. I've been working in the garden, the early autumn sun beating on my bowed back, for a long time. I'm tired and thirsty and definitely not in the mood for yet another of her over-the-top outbursts.

I lower my voice and speak slowly. "Someone's going to get hurt." It sounds like a promise.

"That's the point, Sue." She never calls me Mom anymore. I've told her if she doesn't want to call me Mom, then she doesn't get to call me anything. She knows where the button is that makes my arms, legs and mouth flap. I inhale deliberate, measured breaths – one Mississippi, two Mississippi. She angles the blade tips toward me. "It's your turn to be hurt." Heavy chunks of strawberry-blonde hair hang outside her chaotic ponytail.

I stagger back. The pain I've tried to hide from her kicks back against me. So that was it. She needs to hurt me, her protector, because she doesn't know, because I've hidden my true feelings too well. I've never told her how it felt to find her blacked-out drunk on the living room floor, what it was like to hide her shoes each night so she wouldn't sneak out, or that I vomited when a police officer knocked on our door to say she'd been found beaten and raped the one night I forgot to hide her shoes.

A muscle twitches beneath my eye.

A gaggle of geese squawk overhead, a feathery platoon of drones. The rumble of a postal truck reaches us, and I worry the mail carrier, or a neighbour, or the geese have clued into what is happening. What would an assault charge do to her future?

"This isn't the end of the world," I say.

"Oh my god!" Like a toddler, she stomps her foot. "Give me my phone."

"No," I say.

The smartphone had been a peace offering, her reward for surviving three weeks with underage prostitutes and drug addicts. As we signed the admission form, the director of the youth treatment centre held my shoulder and suggested Cassie's problems were bigger than her father or I could manage. As though we were leaving her at the babysitter, he insisted our goodbyes be quick. Except these babysitters would not be taking her to the park, or reading her Dr Seuss books. Her chin trembled and she battled me away when I tried to hug her. I cried for twenty-one days, but not during parents' night.

If she breaks your house rules, use a currency she understands, we'd heard at our parent support group.

Less than twelve hours into her phone prohibition, and she has already resorted to physical threats, to garden shears. I square my shoulders.

"Dad caught you texting at two this morning." Violation of house rule #26 – no phone calls or texting after eleven. "If you pass your math test, you'll get your phone back."

I chase a look up the street. Although I pray no one is watching, I hope to see one of her sisters coming home.

"I need to talk to my friends." She points her hip at me. The cold look on her sullen face slips and the lines around her mouth soften. For a fleeting moment the little girl who played dress-up with her cat is back. "I won't text after bedtime. I promise," she says, deep dimples appearing on her cheeks.

I sigh and my fists unclench. I'd thought we were good parents. I gave up my career to stay home with my girls. Their father worked sixty hours a week to provide a good life for us. She never had refined sugar before her first birthday cake.

She doesn't get it. "I'm not giving it back. A cell phone is a privilege, not a right." Maybe she'll never get it.

The sweet child vanishes. "It is my right." Oversized

hoop earrings bang against her neck. "I have every right to say goodnight to my friends." She kicks at a chrysanthemum pot, the red one, and it topples. Blood red petals and moist black earth splay away from us.

"They're your friends, not your family," I say, my voice louder than I intend. Last night, I knocked on her door and she told me to fuck off. I put my mouth to the door jam and wished her goodnight. She threw a shoe and the wood panel bounced against my face. I turned the knob and she braced her body against the door. I pushed back. Her feet slid and a sliver of space opened. I sandwiched myself into the gap, and she pressed harder. I avoided looking at the line of bruises on my torso when I showered this morning.

"No, they're my family. You're the people I'm forced to live with." When the therapist asked her younger sister what would be the one thing about our family she'd like to see change she'd answered, that Cassie wouldn't hate her. Her father stays late at work most nights, then every weekend disappears downstairs. He says if he gets too close to Cassie, he might say or do something he'll live to regret. "Give me my phone." She stretches her free hand toward me.

I shake my head.

Her hand and the shears wave between us. "Give me my goddamn phone, right now." My gaze fixes on her and my heart pounds, not because I fear the waving shears, but because I realize, beyond a shadow of a doubt, that she really and truly doesn't trust me. I reach for her.

"Don't." She drops her phone-empty hand and jabs her weapon at me. "Don't you dare touch me."

I pull the garden gloves off, drop them to the ground and surrender my palms to her. Cool air brushes across warmed skin, and the hairs on the back of my hand stand on end.

"Why not help me tidy up this flowerbed?" I ask.

"You don't think I'm serious. You don't think I'd cut you, do you?"

"I think if you hang out here with me, we can talk through what's bugging you."

"I told you what's bugging me. You've got my phone, and I want it back," she says but does lower the shears to her thigh.

I pull the trowel from the dirt and sweep it over the garden. "I thought I'd put these flowers along here, but if you'd rather, you can help me turn over the soil."

"I'm not touching your disgusting muck."

I again stoop to the ground and gather up the gloves. "Put these on," I say.

She considers me a moment, then the gloves. "Then can I have my phone?"

"Maybe," I say.

She places the shears next to her foot, the blade tips pointed away from both of us. Our fingers touch as she takes the gloves. I watch as her doughy soft hands fill first one, then the second deflated glove. "I hate this shit," she says.

"Gardening can be cathartic." I hand her the trowel.

When she and her sisters were younger, I'd squared off three sections in the garden and let each girl decide what to plant in their plot. Cassie asked if she could plant a peanut butter tree. She sulked when her father laughed and told her peanut butter didn't grow on trees. I crouch beside her and begin pulling weeds. The sky changes when a cloud passes above us. With the sun blocked, the air feels more authentic, cooler, more like fall. I tilt my head slightly, just enough to watch her as she works, but not enough that she knows I'm studying her, a sly sideways look. She pays no attention to the goosebumps that have appeared on her arms and legs. She digs a hole, then raises the nearest chrysanthemum, the orange one, out of its pot. The plant leans away from her. The hole is too small, and half the root ball rests above the ground. A groan gurgles in her throat. She brushes loose dirt toward the flower and stands.

"There," she says. "I'll take my phone now."

"You can do better than that. Just set the plant to the side and make the hole a bit bigger."

"I did what you told me to do. I helped you plant your stupid flower. Now give me my phone." The trowel clatters to the ground.

"I'm not giving you the phone unless you finish what you've started." I'm on my feet.

"You lied. You said I could have it if I helped."

"I don't lie."

"Ha," she says. Like an enraged hockey player, she shakes off the gloves.

"Cassandra."

She notices me notice the way her hand is shaking. Fresh tears swim across her eyes.

"You're not perfect. I've heard stories. I know who you really are. I know you did drugs, and I know you were a slag. You're not better than me."

Her words echo through me. I've been found out. When I was seventeen, I'd run away from home. Booze and drugs, plasters to help stop the bleed. Sleeping with every boy who groped under my t-shirt, the only way I could convince myself someone wanted me.

I raise my hand shoulder height. I want to slap her, to stop her from saying anymore, to stop her the way I'd been stopped. My mother had used a wooden spoon, my father a leather belt, an ex-boyfriend, his fists.

She steps closer. "Try it," she says. Her breath puffs into my face, coffee and peanut butter.

I lower my hand. I've never slapped any of my kids.

"Wonder what the neighbours would think about you if they knew the truth?" she asks. Gleeful satisfaction sways across her face. She knows she's rattled me.

My throat tightens. She's too young to understand. She's had an easy life. All the bad that has happened to her, happened because of the poor choices she's made, not because we ever mistreated her, not because we ever rejected her. "I've never used drugs, and I sure never let any boy use me." One day, when she's older, I'll tell her what kind of man her granddad was.

"Liar." Her voice is loud, her words wild again. "I'm done talking." She grabs the rake I've rested against the house. "You don't give a shit about me." A flip of her wrist and the rake is upside down, each metal tine aimed at me. I don't want her to think I'm scared, but for the first time that afternoon, I am. I'm scared for both of us. "You sent me away and I hate you," she says.

She doesn't hate me.

"I love you."

A moment of stillness. The point of return.

"Bullshit," she hisses. My gaze remains steady, unwavering. "Bullshit."

Her facial features twist together, her brow, her lips, her jaw, her eyes. She moves, urgent, crazed, frenzied, a dog lunging for a rabbit.

The point of no return.

My feet won't move, but my torso does. I curl away and fold into myself.

A low whoosh of air as it separates and bangs back together. The tines of the rake catch my sleeve. The tearing sound stops her.

Inside the split-second pause, I glance over my shoulder to see where she is, where the rake is, then it's coming toward me again. Hot pain sears my cheek. My hand covers the opening gashes each tine has made. Her face unfolds and my pain flashes in her eyes. Sticky red seeps between my fingers, blood red. Then a moan, outside of either of us, ascends.

The sound of metal and wood explodes against stone.

She drops to her knees.

I drop to the flagstone.

About the author

Sharon Overend is an award-winning author whose fiction, creative non-fiction and poetry have appeared in Canadian, American and UK literary journals and anthologies. Originally from Toronto, Sharon and her husband now live on a 156-acre property where she has found inspiration for many of her latest writing projects.

www.sharonoverend.blog

The Brothers

Alyson Faye

Lager and lime

Me and Ma stare at the black and white photograph in the faded leather album. "That's your Da and Dom," Ma whispers.

She strokes the glossy image with a shaking finger. Her whole hand shakes now, it's part of her illness.

"They were so strong, so handsome. All the girls in the village wanted to marry them."

"And you got Da and Lizzy got Dom," I finish for her, as Ma gazes around the bedroom, as though she's never seen it before.

In truth she's lived here, in the Bridwood Nursing Home for nearly half a decade.

"They loved a flutter," Ma wheezes. "The dogs, the ponies or…" She is getting tired I can tell.

Da and Dom, twin brothers, born two minutes apart, but as alike as two peas in a pod, rampaging around the sleepy village of Tressick and charming their way through their lives and livelihoods. Da had gone first, in his sleep, and Dom had followed a year later, exactly to the day, which everyone in the village found – inevitable.

I close the photograph album, very very gently, and stroke the surface. It holds so much and it's worn out by the touch of our fingertips.

"Time for bed, Ma." I help her up and walk with her Zimmer towards the bed, smothered with the vintage Paisley duvet, her favourite.

"Night, night," I say. "Sweet dreams."

Ma blinks up at me, from her pillows, child-like and trusting. I kiss her papery cheek, smell her lavender talcum powder. The scent takes me back to my childhood days – of me sitting on the edge of the bed, swinging my legs, whilst Ma got ready to go out for a night out with Da, Dom and Lizzy, and she'd be wearing her best pearl studs and high-heeled black sateen shoes.

I still have the earrings, but Ma broke the heel on one of the shoes running for the night bus to our village and Da carried her home up the hill, even though he'd had a few pints and was staggering all over the place.

Tears prick my eyes, as I'm blind-sided by memories. Looking back – it really hits you in the present.

I close the door, but leave the night-light on. The glow makes Ma look like a caterpillar cocooned – ready to become a butterfly.

Ready to be reborn.

About the author

Alyson's fiction has been published online – most often on the *Horror Tree* site – and in many anthologies. Her work has been read recently on BBC Radio and her latest collection, *Darkness Calls* is out on Amazon.

http://author.to/AlyFayeamazon

Flying Too High

Allison Symes

Strong black tea

So near to the Sun now but unlike Icarus, I was not going to go too high. I knew when to stop. I planned my flight to the last detail. At a certain altitude I would automatically descend so there was no risk of my repeating Icarus's mistake.

I knew better than to let pride get the better of me.

Well, I thought I did.

I am plummeting to earth as I dictate this into my recording machine.

And I realise there was one thing I had forgotten in my haste to prove myself.

I forgot to check nobody else had a chance to interfere with my flying machine.

The last thing I remember seeing before I became airborne was Resbane creeping out of the shed where I kept my device. Resbane who had been dumped by his girlfriend, Strenna, only a day or so ago because she'd found someone new.

That someone new was me.

I guess she will be going back to him after all.

About the author

Allison Symes, who loves quirky fiction, is published by *Chapeltown Books*, *CaféLit*, and *Bridge House Publishing*.

Website: https://allisonsymescollectedworks.com/

Books: http://author.to/AllisonSymesAuthorCent

Her latest flash fiction collection, *Tripping The Flash Fantastic*, is out in Kindle and paperback.

Her *YouTube* channel, with book trailers and story videos, is at www.youtube.com/channel/UCPCiePD4p_vWp4bz2d8o SJA/

FEBRUARY

The authors in this month's selection offer different slants on family relationships.

Making A Perfect Hash of Things *took me back to my own 1950s childhood. A mother's signature dish – "that dreaded midweek staple" – becomes the focal point of a straightforward, loving memoir of childhood.*

In contrast, Jana *depicts a mother reliant on her daughter's paycheck and careless of her welfare. As she searches for her missing daughter during a pandemic, a long inner monologue reveals decades of resentment at being stuck with a "dumb kid". The nameless mother mutters that she will recognise Jana's eyes above a mask, "big blue discs in her crazy head".*

In cryptic snapshots, Flight or Fright *offers insights into what might await a frightened child who faces "a continuous existence of walking on eggshells".*

In Lifesaver, *instinct takes over, and offers a road map for an uncertain future. A modern couple "pitched together in a perfect storm of stress and exhaustion" confront an age-old situation, while bad weather in their holiday location echoes their fractious relationship.*

Lastly, something completely different. Mankind v Tardigrade *provides a salutary reminder that whatever our individual lives hold, complacent humanity may one day be supplanted by indestructible "ugly, wrinkled, eight-legged creatures".*

About the editor

Madeleine McDonald writes flash fiction, radio stories and romance novels. Her work has appeared in *Mslexia* and *The London Reader,* among other journals.

Making a Perfect Hash of Things

Wendy Pike

A cup of hot tea

I love you, despite you making me eat Corned Beef Hash, your signature dish. That dreaded midweek staple you knew I hated. And bitter-tasting Brussels sprouts which my mature tastebuds have since grown to appreciate. Regardless of your insistence my hair must be cut sensibly short, giving me a boy-like appearance instead of the long, feminine locks I longed for, I love you.

Aside from these few nitpicking disagreements, there's nothing about my childhood I'd wish to change. I am blessed. As I grew into adulthood, unwaveringly, you remained my living guardian angel, biggest fan and friend. The best listener on the planet. I really could tell you anything.

It's been seven years since you physically left this world. I now have to make do with the infrequent chances we get to chat – in my dreams. In waking hours I realise there'll be no restorative, reassuring hug. I won't hear you say, "love you lots," as you always did when we parted. But I still feel the force of your nurturing, encouraging, encompassing love, enveloping me like a protective force field. Its depth, warmth and power, along with your imparted wisdom, continue to help me through life's minefields, deflecting much of the bad stuff whenever it heads my way.

Whilst I miss you every day, I'm simultaneously reminded of the most valuable and generous gifts anyone can give and receive. Time and love. And of how lucky I was to have you. Hero and role model, advising, supporting, influencing and inspiring me. I miss us just hanging out together, when we had nothing in particular to do.

I keep talking to you without any expectation of response. If I'm alone, these one-sided conversations are held aloud. So, notwithstanding the Corned Beef Hash, soggy sprouts and dreadful boy's hairdo, which I complained about endlessly at the time, you must know by now Mum, you did a fabulous job and with all my heart I love you lots.

About the author

Wendy Pike writes newsletters and press releases in her day job. In her spare time she enjoys reading and writing creative non-fiction. A few of her life writing tales have previously been published by *CaféLit* where she also has an author page: see it at https://cafelit.co.uk/index.php/meet-our-authors/2-uncategorised/119-wendy-pike

Jana

Elaine Barnard

Cheap white wine

I looked for her everywhere; Jana, my daughter was eighteen when she left. No use contacting police. "She's of age," they'd say. But she's never been of age. She's always been well... how can I say it, backward, shy, challenged?

We'd had an argument, not our usual kind, this was worse. I suspected she'd been seeing someone. She denied it at first, but I knew something was going on. She'd come in from the job she had at 7-11 stocking shelves looking flushed, excited like it was her birthday or something. "Jana," I'd say when she plopped down in front of the TV to watch some late-night horror show, "shouldn't you take a shower and have a bite before bed?" She'd give me that smug look like she had a secret, but she wasn't telling.

"I'm not stupid," I'd say, "something's up. Now get your fat ass into that shower. You smell like that dump you work at."

Jana never answered, just kept her eyes glued to that dumb screen. And speaking of dumb, she sure was. She only finished high school because they pushed her through to get rid of her. They'd spent enough taxpayer dollars trying to educate her, but she was so dense nothing took. "Your daughter's a sweet girl," they'd say at parent conferences. "She just doesn't seem motivated to learn."

I'll motivate her, I'd think, and drag her home, sit her down, open her books and yell, "Now study, damn it." Do you think I was successful? Think again. I wasn't. That's how she ended up at 7-11. But what really began to worry me was when this Pandemic hit. Jana was in the front lines so to speak. No way could she isolate herself. 7-11 needed that merchandise, those shelves of beer and colas, bread, and cookies. Besides, she couldn't afford to stay home. We needed that job. She wasn't eating here for free. No way. Most of her pay went for board and room. What was left she could use for those trashy magazines she stored in her closet. I tried to get rid of them, but she knew every single one. She'd accuse me of stealing which wasn't true. I was just straightening up, so to speak.

Now she's not here I'm concerned not only because I've lost her paycheck which I'd come to depend on but also because of this virus. I mean if she's infected and comes back home, I'd be infected too. We'd both be quarantined. What good would that do us?

So, I started searching every 7-11 I could think of. She wouldn't tell me which one she worked at now. She was constantly being transferred between stores because she was too slow or too tired or the boss didn't like her, or he liked her too much. I put on my mask and drove to the nearest one where I hoped she was still working. I'd recognize her anywhere, mask or not. Her eyes were big blue discs in her crazy head, big blue discs behind bottle glasses. They made her look like ET's sister or some zombie from outer space. When I finally found her, I'd keep my six-foot distance for sure. I'd use the sign language I'd learned to communicate with her after she was diagnosed with a severe hearing loss, not stone deaf but close to it. They found a tumor in her head which they couldn't remove or if they did, she'd be paralyzed, a basket case for certain. I'd be stuck with this vegetable to care for. How fun is that?

It was night when I arrived at 7-11. A few beat up cars in the parking lot. I didn't see her right off, so I went inside to ask the bloated manager if Jana was still working there, stocking shelves in back? He looked at me kinda blank. "Didn't you know?" he said. "Jana had this fever when she came on her shift. I sent her to the ER to get tested for the virus. She's probably still there. If you hurry…"

No way was I going to the Emergency Room. I might get infected myself. Let her quarantine down there. I'm going home and take a hot bath. I'll pour myself some cheap wine and forget I ever had a daughter. But that manager guy came after me. "Hey," he called, "you her mama, right? Well, some dudes were looking for people may have come in contact with her. You need to go down there and get tested too. Probably quarantine you together. Jana's already given them your name."

About the author

Elaine Barnard's collection of stories, *The Emperor of Nuts* was published by *New Meridian Arts* and noted as a unique book on the *Snowflakes in a Blizzard* website. She won first place in Strands International Flash Fiction Competition. Elaine has been nominated for the Pushcart prize and Best Small Fiction. Elaine's second collection, *Fear*, is forthcoming from *Road House Books*.

Fright or Flight

Amanda Jones

Please, just one hot drink

Once again you stand on the doorstep clutching a small bag. What could she need? She looked out onto the street. Dare she? She was little, no more than six years old. That was the first time.

Even then a homeless existence pulled ever more closer. When she was a little older the police came to school to talk and she saw the alcohol and drugs. But what about the lives of the homeless people. They all had lives. Different lives. They had made a choice of flight. Fighting fright or flight.

The alternative was fright.

A continuous existence of walking on egg-shells. Never knowing what the next minute would bring.

Cold, wet nights on doorsteps. Huddled in gutters and urine-stained clothes wrapped around. It was common to see homeless people. One guy was resident on a bench in the park. Sodden cardboard made another shelter in a shop doorway. People walked on by. Nobody gave money to fuel their addictions. And so, nothing was given.

She was around nine years old then.

There was disgust and apprehension in the crowds of oblivion. Packed like ants marching and marching and marching their heads bowed down.

Why didn't they look up?

She never understood.

And so, time and time again, she stood on her doorstep. A limbo between flight or fright. It lasted for what seemed like forever, childhood seemed to take more time than adulthood and days got faster and faster. Her belief stayed her decision. To give up would be to defy God and with prayers every night she could not break a bond of love for Mum. So she stayed and fright or flight was internalised to be physically materialised into a world much later where stress was a proven provocation.

About the author

Amanda has been writing since childhood and along with short stories she writes her Missy Dog charity series, poetry, non-fiction and horror. You can find her here:

Facebook: www.facebook.com/amandababerauthor

Instagram: www.instagram.com/amanda_jones_aka_baber_author

Website: http://amandababerauthor.wordpress.com/

MARCH

The first story I chose was The Girl with the Midas Touch *as it transported me to the Indian village: I could feel the sun and see the colours through the protagonist's eyes when she returned after many years. The themes of jealousy and regret ran through this story.* At 4.00am *intrigued me. Condensed into a hundred words, the menace, tension and relief played with my emotions. The title of* What Happens When You Drink Whiskey during a Retrograde in a Pandemic *drew me in. The thoughts in the girl's mind of good and bad, past and present, longing and loneliness, wanting to remember yet not remember was absorbing. The good memory is tainted; yet she longs to go home. The protagonist is looking backwards, asking for forgiveness yet she is the victim. I chose* Empathy *because it was grief personified. The guilt, the preparations, the waiting, the pretence carries the reader along and it's only at the end we realise the woman is in crisis. It's about kindness and acceptance.* Girl with Dog *is sharply observed and made me rage against the disregard of the girl by the mother. The misery of the girl and the dog is heart-breaking.*

About the editor

Liz Cox lives in the beautiful Yorkshire Dales where she writes short stories and poetry and is about to finish her first novel.

The Girl with the Midas Touch

Nazia Kamali

A mug of hot chocolate

Aaram Bano came to Dehradun after seventeen long years to attend her brother Jamal's granddaughter's wedding, hoping to get a chance to meet the extended family after a long time. The house she had spent her childhood in had changed a lot. An additional storey comprising four bedrooms, a long veranda, and several round pillars whose history was unknown to her had come up. The open courtyard where she used to play had turned into a parlour. The colour of the walls had changed and so had the shapes and sizes of several of its residents.

Aaram loved the gathering. She met several old friends and cousins, and together they reminisced about their childhood. She sang and played *dholki* with the girls and laughed out loud. However, the noise that the younger ones made while dancing to the beats of the latest rock music they played on a full-throated speaker became unbearable after some time. So, giving some trouble to her wobbly knees, she went out of the house in search of a few seconds of peace.

Taking small, steady steps, Aaram walked, observing the changes in the neighbourhood. Buildings, houses, and complexes had come up everywhere, leaving hardly any room for air. New families had shifted to the area. The old landmarks etched so clearly in her memory were nowhere to be found. Most of the previous inhabitants had sold their houses and left. The shops that lined the lanes along which she ran up and down were replaced by modern outlets and convenience stores.

It used to be such a beautiful and spacious locality, she thought.

Aaram Bano hobbled a little further to find the ground where she played with her friends, but it was gone; vanished in the new concrete jungle that had cropped up in the modern times.

Dejected at the loss of her favourite place, she entered the miniscule replica of the playground built around the corner and sat on one of the benches lining its perimeter. There were hardly any trees. Few small swings stood at some distance. At half-past three, the place was almost empty. The late autumn afternoon felt pleasant. Aaram let out an audible breath and peered around.

When she was young, everything looked big and new to her inexperienced eyes. Very few people lived in the neighbourhood. The houses were huge and interspersed. A vast expanse of land was left open after the last one.

Gigantic trees of Mango, Peepal, and Lychee filled the open landscape. A small stream gurgled at its other end.

Women of all ages gathered there for household activities – drying chilies and peppers, making pickles, planning festivities. They would gather in groups and discuss what happened in which household – who was getting married to whom, who disobeyed his parents and ran away from his responsibilities, who spent all the money in vain and who made the most.

Aaram had spent countless hours in that ground. Her happiest memories of childhood were from that place. She and her friends would play all sorts of games – hopscotch, hide and seek, and blind man's bluff. Sometimes the girls would climb high up on the trees and hide, giggling until someone's mother roared at them to come down. They had no gadgets, no fancy toys, and no television sets to glue in front of, yet their hearts were content.

The quiet in the place was welcoming. Aaram closed her eyes and rested her back as the brisk breeze transported her back to the time when she was one hell of a runner. No one in the entire neighbourhood could defeat her until Nimra came along – three years her junior and already as tall as her at the age of ten.

That girl broke every rule set upon them by the elders. Her unkempt, long hair, hung loose instead of being tied up in tight plaits like the rest of them. Though she wore *salwar kameez* and slippers like everyone else, most of the time, her slippers were of different colours or sizes as if she had left home in a hurry and wore anything she found. She rubbed fruits that fell from the trees upon her *kameez* and ate them without washing. When any older girl scolded her for the deed, she stuck out her tongue in defiance. She feared no one and usually played alone, starting one game after the other spontaneously – now she is climbing the tree, and just a second later, she jumped into the stream, splashing water all around. There was nothing predictable about her except the fact that she was a winner.

Running was the most popular sport with girls their age. They had to run and touch the Peepal tree standing at one end of the ground and then return to the starting point. Chatty as she was, Nimra always started late, being busy talking with a friend; and was often last to touch the tree. However, she never finished second. Every time Aaram smiled inwardly when Nimra reached the tree after her, the girl would beat all others and win. She was swift as an arrow and dashed past her competitors without a moment's notice.

Aaram began loathing her. There was no minute, no second when she did not hate the girl. Nimra, on the other hand, was oblivious to all that hatred and jealousy. She had no desire to please anyone. An air of nonchalance surrounded her at all times. She never followed the herd of girls; instead, she came and went all around the neighbourhood as she liked.

Aaram had often seen her play all by herself in the middle of summer afternoons when the sun shone mightily. She hated Nimra's guts and yet admired the ease with which she carried herself.

As they grew up from little girls to young teenagers, everything that Nimra touched turned into gold. Every person she met fell in love with her.

Nimra became tall and thin with full lips and big brown eyes that had a language of their own, while Aaram remained short and carried a tadpole belly. There was nothing extraordinary about her looks, and every time she looked at Nimra, she wished for something bad to befall her. Whenever the girl dressed herself up for any occasion, it became impossible for people to tear their eyes away from her. Aaram hated the attention they paid to her.

Wherever there was a gathering in the neighbourhood, her name echoed.

So young and yet so smart.

Does math far beyond her age.

Have you seen the bed sheet she embroidered recently?? So beautiful. Such exquisite design.

I wonder how a girl her age is able to manage such precision.

Aaram's life became an unending competition with a girl who didn't even bother to enter into one with her. She tried doing everything that Nimra was praised for – she studied her elder brother's book and painted a bunch of flowers on the cushion covers, she imitated her laughter and nonchalance during ceremonies but nothing seemed to work, or maybe it did but to Aaram, it was never as good as her adversary.

She spent hours and hours going over detailed plans to defeat Nimra, dotting every "i" and crossing every "t" meticulously – how she would run with all her might in the next race and beat Nimra, or how she would embroider an elaborate and intricate pattern on one of the bed sheets to impress every woman in the neighbourhood. She became obsessed with the idea of excelling, of going far and beyond to claim victory over the girl.

And then came Sarmad.

The local doctor's son, who studied in Delhi, returned one summer after passing out of high school. Aaram saw him from the terrace of her house as he walked with long confident strides on the road outside. It was love at first sight. His glorious aura captivated her, and the entire summer, she could see nothing but Sarmad all around. Every corner she looked, she saw him – standing, sitting, smiling, laughing, talking, eating, and walking. He had captured her senses until one day when the news of his elopement with Nimra reached her ears.

Aaram's insides were set on fire. That girl was bad news since day one. She had stolen everything from her, everything. A blanket of hatred enveloped her as she ran away, hiding tears of dejection.

Soon she married and moved to Saharanpur.

Whenever she came to see her parents, Aaram asked after Nimra, and to her dismay, there was always something good going on in her life – Sarmad came back and apologised to his parents who accepted their union after all. He went to a medical school. Their firstborn was a son. They had four children together. Sarmad named his clinic after Nimra.

She would listen to everything and think that all this would have been hers had that girl not come in between. It took Aaram decades to forgo that feeling.

For the past several years, she hadn't thought about Nimra at all. It was only after reaching Dehradun, that she remembered the girl with long unkempt hair and big brown eyes. Upon asking, she was told, that Nimra passed away seven years ago. Sarmad followed soon after. A tinge of hatred showed itself in Aaram's eyes as she imagined them together in the heavens. The girl's Midas touch worked even in death. She rested in the hereafter not alone but with the love of her life.

Now, as she sat on the bench and recalled everything and then she realised that she would never see Nimra again, never hear her voice. The girl did not breathe anymore. She didn't share the sun and the moon with her any longer…

Despite sun still being there in the sky, the air felt chilly, she rubbed the nape of her neck and then crossed her arms tightly. A feeling of emptiness seemed to be closing in from all sides. A loud gasp escaped her mouth.

Aaram suddenly longed for her rival – to run up to the aging peepal tree and lose to her in the race once again, to see her play those spontaneous games and never bother to include others. She longed for the touch of her warm hands and the smile on her soft baby-like face that never failed to enrich those oval eyes of hers. Aaram wished to see her outdo everyone else by her wit and intelligence one more time.

Tears flowed from her eyes onto her cheek, making their way to her chin and hence the lap as she realised after seventy long years that she had never hated the girl.

About the author

Nazia lives in Dehradun, a small valley in the Himalayas. Her work has been published in *FemAsia, The Indian Periodical, Rigorous, In Parentheses,* and several other magazines. Her novella is all set to appear in the annual anthology by *Running Wild Press.*

What Happens When You Drink Whiskey During a Retrograde in a Pandemic

Riham Adly

Middle Eastern Sahlab drink

March 9th, 2020

Dear Diary,

They still haunt me to this day: pistachios and rosewater – Mama's constant ingredients. Their scents absent from my everyday life yet forever omnipresent. They are particularly strong today like pain in a limb that's no longer there. Perhaps because Mercury's gone retrograde? It really makes no difference. I've been moving backwards ever since I set foot in this new country, this foreign city, this absent existence.

The whiskey tastes like piss! I curse this bastard lung-sucking covid-19 of a virus as my chest tightens.

Outside the window, the women and men rushing into the subway in spite of the freezing cold no longer exist. The smell of coffee spilling from Nino's Café is also long gone. No clamor, no car-horns, no busy streets.

It seems absence is quite a thing right now.

I stare at the useless plane ticket and the useless brochures sitting on the antique coffee table I dragged all the way from home, decades ago.

Will they ever take me back?

A long healthy swig of the piss-tasting whiskey

warms my throat and numbs the pain that's been growing slow and huge like the pots of pistachio and rosewater pudding Mama used to make back in the day when Baba came back from his travels.

Will they ever forgive me?

Moth-eaten images I tried so hard to banish from my memory resurface: the ice-cream shop in Aleppo around the corner from our house where I used to slip unseen for the clementine-flavored boza. I try to shoo them away like the pesticide-resistant flies that won't leave me alone.

The boy serving the ice-cream had eyes the color of Mama's pistachios and…

I don't. Want. To remember!

He wasn't really a boy, rather a young man of nineteen, with firm hands that gripped mine whenever handing me the treats I asked for.

You should've seen it coming. The hiss of my indrawn breath startles my ears.

I can still hear the listening silence inside the elevator, and feel the firm grip of those warm hands pushing me into a corner. I had just started bleeding last month, before that I was never really aware of that place between my legs. His thrusts were quick and precise, not one moment wasted on unneeded thrills. Ironically, it happened only hours before my Hijab-wearing initiation. On that day, the women of the family made sure I understood that chastity was this family's most valuable currency.

Years later, after the forced wedding I ran away from to my permanent exile here in New York City, the ice-cream boy sent anonymous letters with weighted words like rape, and regret. My desperate mother had probably given him the address.

I feel sick and throw up all over my passport and the picture of Wadi Kandeel Beach on the travel brochure, but a cold gust escapes the window bringing along with it the dazzle of yellow morning light. At this point, I realize I want some sunshine.

I just want the beach and the sun. Any beach and any sun, Aleppo, New York, it doesn't really matter.

About the author

Riham Adly is a Best of the Net and Pushcart Prize nominee. Her work has appeared in over fifty online journals such as *Litro, Lost Balloon, The Flash Flood, The Citron Review, The Sunlight Press, Flash Frontier* and *Flash Back* among others. Her work is included in *Best Micro-fiction 2020.*

At 4.00 am

P. A. Westgate

A gulp of rough red wine

At 4.00 am blood pressure and body temperature are at their lowest and the risk of death is at its maximum. They say that more people die at 4.00 am than at any other time. At 4.00 am you're lying in bed, your stomach in knots, praying that an unguarded remark hasn't been reported. This is when you hear cars screeching to a halt in the street and heavy boots on the staircase. When you hear hammering on the door and harsh voices, 4.00 am is when you thank God that it's someone else's door this time and not yours.

About the author
P. A. Westgate is an enthusiastic but sporadic writer. He lives quietly in his native Essex.

Empathy

Swati Moheet Agrawal

Ristretto

Every Sunday my wife rises from bed like someone with purpose. Her energy levels are alarmingly phenomenal that day of the week. However, as the day begins to wane, her enthusiasm takes a nosedive faster than it surges through every cell in her being.

Her mother promises to come over for dinner every Sunday but fails to show up.

My wife washes the linen herself. Never mind that the sheets are freshly laundered, reeking of detergent, soft and warm. She spends half the day sprucing up the house: she runs a rag along every corner, painstakingly and diligently, rearranges furniture with great gusto, changes cushion covers, strings marigold to make a bright garland for the front door, burns incense, puts out her best china, lays out the block printed set of 6 *Kalamkari* placemats her mother specially fetched for her from Jaipur, and so and so forth.

Get a dozen *rajbhogs*, she orders Raju to get her mother's favourite sweet dish from the bazaar. Raju, our man Friday, indulges her just the same. We know the drill.

The dinner table is laden with hors d'oeuvres like *achari paneer* and *aalo chaat*. Main course comprises of her mother's favourite black *dal* and steamed rice, *naan*, and mixed vegetable among other delicacies.

The blue goes out of the sky, the green slips away from the trees, everything dwindles away into darkness and the day finally fades away.

It is half past eleven. We are still waiting at the dinner table.

My wife retreats to a corner to call her mother. She hangs up after a few minutes.

Mummy has promised to come home next Sunday, she tells me rather sheepishly.

Raju dutifully winds up the kitchen. I lovingly put my wife to sleep.

My mother-in-law died of a cardiac arrest last year. She was really on her way home for dinner that Sunday.

Glossary

Aloo chaat – An Indian savoury snack served with potatoes, sauces and spices.

Achari paneer – Tangy, flavorful cottage cheese appetizer.

Dal – Lentils, a staple ingredient in Indian cuisines.

Kalamkari – A traditional Indian art form involving block printing or hand painting, usually done on cotton fabrics.

Naan – Flatbread.

Rajbhog – Saffron-flavored cottage cheese dumplings, an Indian dessert, stuffed with exotic dry fruits.

About the author

Swati Moheet Agrawal is a poet and writer whose work has appeared in *Sledgehammer Lit, Modern Literature* and *Thimble Lit Mag* among other journals. When not buried in books, she dabbles in decoupage art.

Girl with Dog

Lesley James

Dry Martini, stirred not shaken

She had to make the perfect picture, in order to demonstrate that She Was Doing It Right. She hired an official photographer. He circled the birthday party guests, snapped blowing out the candles and cake-eating and posed chaotic six-year-olds in a few shots here and there.

She had pinned the girl's hair tight to her head in an effort to restore the baby curls, long gone. The Pocket Beagle puppy birthday present arrived by train from Cornwall, in a label-plastered tea-chest, having bitten the guard on the journey. A hand scrawled note: "Vicious dog inside", was stapled to the top of the crate.

And the chicken-pox pock-marked child sat, still as a painting, with the tiny dog in her lap. "For God's sake, try to look grateful," said her mother between cigarettes. "None of your pussy cat smiles." She could have been talking to the dog who cowered, petrified. No-one had ever heard of a Pocket Beagle. The girl hadn't asked for a dog. Both girl and dog were too tiny and frightened to enjoy the party much. They looked at each other in shared misery.

Over the shoulder to an aunt: "Did I tell you that

she invited the whole bloody class? Several of the invitations had to be cancelled."

Another cigarette. "And that guitar birthday cake? I ask you, only *she* would want a guitar! Well, that's never happening again. I've worked my fingers to the bone..."

Among her things, when we cleared the house after she died, we found thirty-two identical black and white, pristine card-mounted photos of the girl with the dog.

On her fifteenth birthday, the girl bought herself a guitar.

About the author

Lesley is a writer and teacher. She was shortlisted for Love Reading UK's 2022 very short story prize. She has prose and poetry for adults in *The Broken Spine*, *Roi Fainéant* and *Full House Lit Mag*. Poetry for children can be found in *Parakeet Magazine* and *The Dirigible Balloon*.

APRIL

At a time when our world was still slowly starting to emerge from travel restrictions and lockdown, the April stories showered us with watery visits to the sparkling Boulick Stream and learning to be a life guard at Lake Harriet, as well as thoughts on hand-gel and yellow custard. Heart-felt responses were shown to Covid, from a moving nursing home story, to the rousing analogy of washing hands. There's some poetry inspired prose, with D.H. Lawrence's poem, Snake, *winding in and out of the narrative, and a reality focused poem. All four pieces considered relationships and new ways to care.*

About the editor
Linda Flynn has had books published for children and teenagers, as well as short stories for adults. Her anthology, *I Knew it in the Bath*, will be released in September 2022 with *Bridge House Publishing*. She can be found at: www.lindaflynn.com

To the Scald a Salve after *Snake* by D.H. Lawrence

Maura Barrett

Mead

By ancient stone walls in stolen away places, clandestine. Shadows splayed on limestone towers; sunlight sparkled on the Boulick stream. He a Pharos, to which I was drawn, lured by the corona of his eclipse. He liked the reflection, how it shimmered "on a hot, hot day". My vessel glides serene, assured, rose tresses in my wake. He rested a soft-cover book against the sill of a stone arch and cited verses. I consumed his stance; his mystery and I inhaled the breath that he exhaled and tingled alive. Listened and "like a second comer" waited. His foot rested on "a fissure in the earth-wall" solid. High above in a cloudless sky, a pair of swallows spiralled in elegance.

"Was it perversity that I longed to talk to him? Was it humility, to feel so honoured? I felt so honoured." There was something in how he held his wrist, in how his unbuttoned shirt sleeve revealed a filigree of capillaries and soft skin. There was something too in how he fingered his hair shyly, unconsciously, his eyes gentle and cordial, noble yet mischievous. The literature or rather his delivery of the poem, enticed me like fairy music. Perhaps he was the King of the Sidhe, for what was in him was potent and primal, "earth-golden from the burning bowels of the earth".

There was between us a channel of ionised air charged with a current that fizzed. I knew it in an instant. Knew by the tone in his voice when he spoke with me in the mill "and mused a moment", by how he leant his hand against the wall behind me and "looked at me vaguely", and by the scent of him. Lightning strikes aged walls and grounded and all as I was, it scorched me. Then there was the hand of providence, meeting in unexpected places, reaching for the same book, the hook of history, the love of words. And so began my enchantment.

Trifling with the fairies is never wise. I of all people knew this and we had promises to keep. So I donned my warp shield and kept it in check and he shrouded me in a woollen brat. Once he morphed into a horned stag and I was very nearly lost. I had to dig deep, source the strength from the core of me, unleash those uncharted waters by way of defence. Each time I quelled it, it depleted my resolve. "And voices in me said, if you were a man you would take a stick and break him now". The woman in me, responded to the man in him "and yet those voices" and the contradiction seared me. "But must I confess how I liked him, how glad I was he had come like a guest in quiet, to drink at my water-trough."

So that is how we went on, surviving intact

somewhere in the midst of contradiction. "And truly I was afraid, I was most afraid, but even so, honoured still more that he should seek my hospitality from out the dark door of the secret earth". Time mulled along. Catastrophes happened, lives changed. I hid from his gaze a while, seeking refuge in the shade. Wondrous things happened and in the joys we celebrated, ever mindful, ever careful, ever drawn. And in those times he quenched his thirst "he drank enough and lifted his head, dreamily, as one who has drunken" and I imbibed in the honour of keeping that pitcher replenished. Paradoxically the more he consumed the more intoxicated I became. Then he faced the heart of darkness "and looked around like a God, unseeing, into the air, and slowly turned his head" and left me.

"A sort of horror, a sort of protest against his withdrawing into that horrid black hole, deliberately going into the blackness" found a home in me. "And I thought of the albatross and I wished he would come back" and a spell later he did, Fate sending out her tendrils to snare us. By more ancient walls on the Shannon shore, I invoked the Goddess Sionna in her wisdom as my guide. My well spring was as arid as the deserts of the heart of darkness, and I could divine no more. She sent us wine and she sent us sunlight and she sent us the hook of history.

Somewhere on that quest, on the boundary of a townland we crossed a line and "suddenly that part of him that was left behind convulsed in undignified haste writhed like lightning, and was gone." Being slighted made me harsh and I spat curses in his wake. It was a fury begot in rejection and rancour and I banished the Sun Deity, who cited me verses.

"Don't contact me ever again!"

I stomped away intact; my flag of righteous victory unfurled trailed after me. Joan of Arc, Bodecia, Maeve, "and immediately I regretted it, I thought how paltry, how vulgar, what a mean act!" I despised myself and the voices. The flames followed, licking, searing, scorching. I curled the flag around me, wounded and hurt and settled into a mire of anger, a morass so laden and shrouded in mists of wrath that no sun would pierce it. He was gone "pacified, and thankless" and good riddance.

Until thirty moons on, the night of a super moon eclipse, when planet and satellite and sun tug and play light against shadow. The Moon in her dance exudes sapience. The Earth tilts in homage and the Sun's fire soothes not seers, balms are born. At once "he seemed to me again like a king, like a king in exile, uncrowned in the underworld, now due to be crowned again."

Somewhere by a window in a Celtic night, a woman sits, moon shadows on a freckled face, rose hair soft on her back. She looks into the night, and wonders. She marvels at how light it feels to have laid down the burden of resentment, the power of hate.

Her scald is salved. She wishes him well and sends him good thoughts to waft on his crinkled face in gentleness and in light and in love, penetrating the heart of darkness where she thinks he might be. She hopes that on the turn of the axis mundi that they might reach him, on this special night.

"And so, I missed my chance with one of the lords of life. And I have something to expiate: A pettiness."

About the author

Maura Barrett is an emerging Irish writer who grew up in the Comeragh Mountains. She believes that there is a language in landscape that seeps out of her and fires her imagination. It is sprinkled with metaphor; the ordinary, everyday event trickles out and tells the deeper story.

I Wish You Were Closer

Tony Domaille

Camp coffee

"I wish you were closer," she said.

I put my palm to the Perspex screen between us and watched her raise her own frail, wrinkled, hand to meet mine. Close, but still a world away.

"Are you eating?" she asked. "You look like you could do with a few decent meals. Do you remember my hot pot?"

I smiled. If anyone could do with feeding up it was her. The care home manager said she lived on hope and custard. The hope that someone would visit and give her a hug, and custard because it required no chewing. They tried to persuade her to eat, but she just nibbled a little, pushed her plate away, and begged for the yellow stuff that kept her going.

"You should try to eat better," I said.

She shrugged. "I would if you sat down with me."

She knew I couldn't. Even though the pandemic was waning, the closest I could be was the other side of this screen, though I wondered if the kitchen would allow us to have a plate each here. I wasn't hungry, but I was prepared to match her, fork for fork, with some lasagne or cottage pie, or whatever they served up to the dentally challenged.

I would have suggested it, but she launched into

her stories. Way back in time when I did things that made her laugh or cry or proud. I watched her eyes light up as her memories flooded back, one after another. I had groomed the dog with garden shears. I had flooded the bathroom playing submarines. I had won school prizes, been kind, had the finest wedding day she had ever known, and been the best son a mother could ever wish for.

"You've always been a lovely boy," she said, putting her palm to the screen again.

I mirrored her hand. "You're lovely yourself."

And then the care worker was there behind her, tapping at his watch and mouthing that it was time I was leaving.

She looked tearful when I said I had to go. "I wish you were closer," she said again.

I blew her a kiss in return for the one she blew me and watched as she was led away back to her room.

As I signed myself out at reception the care home manager said to me, "Thank you for coming. Mary so looks forward to your visits."

"Does anyone else visit at all?" I asked.

"Not a soul, so you volunteers are a godsend," said the manager. But I suppose she knew what I was thinking because then she said, "Dementia isn't always a curse, it can sometimes be a curse, but it can also be a blessing. Mary thinks you're her son, doesn't she?"

About the author

Tony has written a number of award-winning plays, published by *Lazy Bee Scripts* and *Pint Sized Plays*, that have been performed across the world. He has also had many stories published in anthologies and magazines. You can follow him here:
www.facebook.com/tonydomaillewriting/

Zinc

Jim Bates

Ice water

The head of Parks and Recreation, Fred Nicoletti, extended his hat. "Good luck, kid, he winked. "You're going to need it."

Nothing like a little intimidation to add to my already jangling nerves. I was standing on the north beach of Lake Harriet, getting ready for my final test. I'd passed the written part of the exam fine, just like last year. But now came the hard part. Each of us aspiring newbies had to rescue one of the senior life guards to prove ourselves worthy of this coveted summer job.

Last year, the name I'd pulled out of the hat was a guy named Ben who everyone called Bronko. He looked like a bronco. He was stocky and hairy and incredibly strong. When I swam out to attempt a rescue, I tried to put him in a cross chest carry and get him moving to shore. It didn't work. He just kept rolling over and over with skinny little me hanging on for dear life. I couldn't stop him. Finally, Nicoletti, who'd been watching the pathetic spectacle from shore blew his whistle.

"That's enough." He waved us in. I walked up to him, panting and trying to catch my breath. He just smirked and shook his head to the negative, making it a point of crossing my name off the list. "Can't have the person drowning drown the rescuer, Jakobson," he said. The rest of the life guards laughed at his joke. "See ya' around."

I rode my bike home, vowing to come back next year. Why? Well, that was the big question, wasn't it? Why would I want to put myself through that embarrassing experience again? Bronko could have drowned me if he'd wanted. The best answer I could come up with was that maybe it was just a guy thing. Something I had to prove to myself.

My older brother was exceptionally coordinated and excelled at sports. He was good looking, popular, well liked and had lots of friends, all traits I didn't even come close to sharing with him. I was short and skinny and it seemed like I had been wearing glasses pretty much my whole life. Not a lot of friends, either. I did well in school, though, there was that. And I liked to swim.

Two winters before, I had passed my senior life saving test so I could become a life guard, but as I said, failed the "rubber meets the road" test last summer. I hoped this year would be different, but still didn't have a good answer as to why. Even to this day. I've told this story to my wife, and when I mention the "guy thing" to her, she just shakes her head. "That's so sad, Soren. It's just so sad."

And I have to agree with her that it is. Now. But back then, I felt I had something to prove.

With Fred Nicoletti standing over me, winking away like a crack addict, I extended my shaking hand to the hat and pulled out a folded piece of paper. I unfolded it, read the name and handed it to him. "Damn," I muttered.

Nicoletti read it, laughed and turned to where Lou Dobson, the biggest of this year's crop of life guards, was standing, and yelled, "Hey, Big Lou. Got yourself an easy one."

Big Lou, to his credit didn't say anything in return. He just looked at me, smacked a mouthful of bubble gum, and saluted.

Where Bronko had been short, round and hairy, Lou was tall and muscular. To me he looked like I imagined Hercules would have. Only bigger, stronger and better looking. *God,* I thought to myself, *I'm done for.*

To begin the test, Big Lou swam out about fifty yards from shore and motioned for me to come get him. I waded into the water up to my waist and then started doing the breast stroke. As I approached, my pretend victim started thrashing around, kicking and splashing and swinging his arms, acting like he was drowning.

I knew exactly what to do. I got within ten feet, dove and swam under water to him. I grabbed his waist and twisted him so he was facing away from me. Then I ladder walked my hands up his sides, gripping him as strong as I could to hold onto him. And, surprise, as opposed to last year, this time I gained control. I was giving myself a silent congratulations, when all of a sudden he tried to turn on me. I held firm, broke the surface and with his back to me reached over his chest and secured him in a cross chest carry with my right arm.

I held tight and used my left arm to pull myself and him through the water toward shore, scissor kicking for all I was worth. After a minute, it dawned on me something miraculous was happening. It was working. I was actually rescuing Big Lou.

As I neared shore, I noticed he was becoming awfully limp. *He's doing a great job pretending*, I thought. I moved forward for a few more strokes before having another thought. A horrific one. I was close enough to shore that I could stand. I let go of Lou and looked at him floating on his back. He was turning blue. I quickly checked and determined he wasn't breathing. My first thought was maybe something was stuck in his throat.

I turned and yelled for help. Then I lifted him out of the water, facing me and over my shoulder. I slammed him hard on the back. Once. Twice. And on the third smack I felt him cough, and then cough again. I lay him down on his back and watched as color returned to his face. I checked and he was breathing okay. He was going to be all right.

As I held him floating, I saw a big wad of gum floating in water. That's what I'd pounded out him.

If it hadn't been for me, he would have choked on the damn thing. That's what everyone told me afterward, anyway.

There were thirty candidates for the five life guard jobs that summer, and I got one of them. After I was hired, Lou kind of took me under his wing. One of the first things he did was give me a tube of zinc oxide.

"You'll need this for the sun, Sorenski." Yeah, that was his nickname for me. I didn't mind. He was a good guy. He even fixed me up on a double date with him and his girlfriend. My first date ever. He turned me on the Motown music, gave me my first joint and all and all didn't mind that I was a geeky kid with glasses. I appreciated that in him. A lot.

That following fall, Lou enlisted in the army. He was sent to Vietnam and was killed at Khe Sanh in early 1968. By then I was attending the University of Minnesota and had a deferment so I was safe from the draft. I went to his funeral. A lot of us former life guards were there, even Fred Nicoletti. I'd grown my hair long and had a wispy beard. He recognized me, though, and said, "Hey there Sorenski."

"How's it going?" I asked. I really didn't have much to say to him.

"Hell of a thing, isn't it?" He said, pointing at the flag draped casket. "Hell of a thing."

"It is," I agreed with him.

"You take care." He clapped me on my shoulder and walked away.

Right then and there, the summer when I'd been a life guard with Lou, the one up until then I'd thought of as the best summer of my life, seemed a long way away. Almost like it never had happened. But it had, not only the job, but my friendship with Lou. And for that I'll always be grateful.

About the author
Jim lives in a small town twenty miles west of Minneapolis, Minnesota. His stories and poems have appeared in nearly three hundred online and print publications. *Resilience*, a collection of short stories, was published in February, 2021 by *Bridge House Publishing*. Additional stories can be found on his blog:
www.theviewfromlonglake.wordpress.com.

With Your Hands

Anne Goodwin

Neat alcohol distilled from hand sanitiser

When this is over, will you remember
How you spilled from your shelters
Paused on your doorsteps
To pledge your support
Your loyalty and gratitude
With your hands?

When there's a vaccine, will you fondly recall
How, primed by the press,
You joined with your neighbours
(Though socially distanced

In your separate booths)
You fisted your pens
You carved your crosses
For the white man who promised
To combat the virus
Of handholds and handouts,
Through immunisation from sharing, from caring, from mingling
With those who had drawn life's short straw?

#

When your hairdresser's bruised
At the hands of her husband—
Because the children were whingeing
And he'd drunk the last lager
And there's nowhere to hide in a one-bedroom flat—
Will you glamorise your garden
Pluck out the weeds
Clip the first roses
To arrange in a vase
With your hands?

When your cleaner's collapsed
In the queue for the food bank—
Having spent six months' rent
On renewing the visa
To legally wipe Covid from hospital toilets—
Will you rub fat into flour
Beat eggs into sugar
With a whisk, with a spoon, with your hands?

When the rainbows have faded
Will your darlings want answers
As to why crucial contracts
For masks, gowns and testing
Were tenderly handed without competition
To party patrons and profiteers?

When scapegoating yo-yos
Between experts and migrants,

You-name-it minorities and benefit scroungers,
Will you tut at the tabloids
As you pay for your croissants
Then trot to your car
And squirt sanitiser onto your hands?

#

When Brand Boris-Being-Boris
Is your after-dinner speaker
Will you clap for old Eton
For boisterous Bullington
For the bow ties and tailcoats
That hot-house debaters, optimists, egotists
Who chart the death toll with their hands?

When Parliament cycles
To another election
And you enter the booth,
Will your violence seem distant,
Self-interest more urgent,
Or will you discover
The power of your hands
To spread kindness
Compassion
Fairness
Community?

Will you repair
The damage you did with your hands?

About the author

Anne Goodwin's debut novel, *Sugar and Snails* was shortlisted for the 2016 Polari First Book Prize. Her second novel, *Underneath*, appeared in 2017 and her short story collection, *Becoming Someone,* in 2018. Her third novel, *Matilda Windsor Is Coming Home*, was published in May, 2021. A former clinical psychologist, Anne is also a book blogger specialising in fictional therapists.

Website: http://annegoodwin.weebly.com

Twitter @Annecdotist

TikTok: @annegoodwinauthor

MAY

I liked the starkness of Isolation Day 1483, *with its short sentences and depiction of monotony. I could feel the narrator's boredom, then the flicker of pleasure that something as small as a fly could bring, before he settled into yet another day of the same.*

The Boy With the Van *reminded me of visits to my great aunt, not knowing whether she would remember me but then listening to her stories from the past, told in great detail. The reminiscences in this story are beautifully expressed and the ending moved me deeply.*

I think a lot of people will relate to Unstoppable You *– an immediate "yes" from me. It is told in the second-person point of view, cleverly putting the reader in the narrator's post-lockdown shoes. It was impossible not to empathise.*

Teehee, Busy Bee. *It is a fun little story that made me chuckle at the end. There's your warning, people; don't live on Zoom!*

I chose An Unexpected Visitor *because it shows real understanding of the emotional realm and complexity of grief, which is particularly moving to readers who have lost someone close to them. It was sad and comforting, simultaneously, finishing on a hopeful note.*

About the author
Hannah Retallick, writer and editor from North Wales.

www.hannahretallick.co.uk/

Isolation Day 1483

Kevin Wood

Water (with a piece of stale bread)

Isolation. Day One Thousand, Four Hundred and Eighty-Three. Another day. And yet every day is the same. Here surrounded by the same four walls.

To my left is small window where sometimes shafts of sunlight glint through in the morning. To my right a window where the sun may appear later in the day. Today there is no sun. Just grey. And cold.

I busy myself doing trivial tasks. But tasks that are now important parts of the day to me. I read. I read a lot more than I used to. I touch each of the four walls in turn as if tenderly caressing them. Like I am sending a message to them. I am still here. I will often walk around the darkened room.

I've started counting how many times I do these things each day. Some days I do this more than others. On other days I just stare impassively at the walls. I often imagine the wall in front of me. I imagine my friends are standing by it. Sometimes I smile at them. Sometimes I talk to them. Sometimes they answer me. Sometimes they don't.

As the minutes turned into hours something appeared to disturb me. Something crossed my eyeline. Startled I tried to focus on where this object seemed to have gone to in the room. It was a fly. Its flight was random as it moved to and fro around the room. After a while It settled above me on the ceiling.

I smiled. It brought me some relief to watch it as it moved around. It was a happy distraction that helped to break up the monotony of the day. The appearance of my flying friend had served this purpose.

The sun is shining through the window to my right now.

Soon the day will be over. Another day will be done. Another day alone. Tomorrow will be another day.

Isolation. Day One Thousand, Four hundred and Eighty-Four.

About the author

Kevin Wood is a retired Accountant from Basildon, Essex and has been writing short stories since his retirement. These stories often portray the bleakness and desperation of the characters' lives.

The Boy with the Van

Emma Robertson

Tequila Sunrise

It was the snatched hint of a song, emanating tinnily from someone's phone as they passed the door, that made me think again of the boy, the beautiful boy with the translucent skin and hazel eyes. *Mellow Yellow*; I haven't heard it in years. It made me think of all the long-haired boys of my youth, but that one in particular. I wish I could remember his name.

There's no music in here other than the arhythmical beeping of machines and the occasional soft shoe shuffle of passers-by. My breathing, amplified by the – whatever it is – on my face creates a two-time beat of sorts, but not one you could dance to. I sing the song to myself in my head to pass the time and conjure up the memory of the boy I'd loved when I was a girl.

He'd had a van, I recall. We used to go all over, listening to bands, and then make love for hours in the back of it. He had this awful purple rug; I laugh now at the thought of it, as much as anyone can laugh with all this gear on their face, but it had seemed so cool then. Lit by the psychedelic glow of a lava lamp, the air infused with the sweet aroma of joss sticks and spliffs, I'd consider it an assault on the senses now, not to mention a fire hazard, but for teenage me, it was paradise, as long as he was there.

George, that was his name, I remember now. He'd had that narrow-hipped androgynous look that was so fashionable at the time, all eyes and lips, pretty as a peach but masculine with it. I was so skinny myself then, he used to pour dribbles of wine into the hollow above my clavicle and sip it slowly, stopping every now and then to look me right in the eye, as if drinking in my very soul.

I remember the birthmark on the back of his hand, shaped like a swallow in flight. I used to stroke it and wonder what would become of us. My mother constantly warned me that a man like that wouldn't stay around for long, that I should find a nice boy with good prospects. "Excitement's all well and good, but excitement doesn't pay the bills," said the woman who, I was convinced, had never experienced a moment's excitement in her life.

The nurse's voice brings me back to the present. "Mrs Morris. George is here to see you."

My heart leaps, wondering if my daydreams have somehow manifested themselves until I see that it's just some old man, not the boy from my memories. "Hello love," says the stranger.

I ignore him, too disappointed to answer.

The nurse sighs. I hear her say to the old man, "She has good days and bad days," before turning to me again. "Mrs Morris." She raises her voice. "Your husband has come to see you."

He places his hand over mine and I spot the faded shape of a swallow in flight.

About the author

Emma Robertson is a dance tutor and writer from London, UK. Her pieces can be found in literary magazines and flash fiction collections including *Ellipsis Zine*, *Lunate* and *Funny Pearls*, as well as in several anthologies. She was recently longlisted for the Bath Flash Fiction Award and will appear in their 2022 collection published later this year.

Unstoppable You

Laura Cody

Flat seltzer

You linger an extra five minutes over your second cup of coffee, luxuriating in the quiet house after what virtually amounted to fourteen months of prison time in G-pop. With friends, you pay dutiful lip-service to the hidden blessings of the pandemic, the silver linings behind the sorrows. You say it taught you to slow down, to enjoy simple pleasures – a home-cooked meal, a jigsaw puzzle, a socially-distanced stroll in fading sunlight. You don't mention how your house shrunk to the dimensions of a tuna can, how your husband set up his work-from-home office in the dining room, so his voice boomed throughout the house all day on videoconferences, how it became impossible to exit or leave without his notice, how you couldn't enter the kitchen for a nibble without his head bobbing over your shoulder to see what you were eating. You don't talk about how your three kids staked out personal territories in the house with all the don't-cross-this-line menace of schoolyard bullies, how you were relegated to a "home office" in the corner of your bedroom, essentially a small desk next to the bathroom.

You put the empty coffee cup in the dishwasher, and savor the solitude. Your husband went back to his real office, kids to in-person school. You, yourself, are heading back tomorrow.

But you have today.

One day to remedy fourteen months of self-neglect. There will be a run, a shower and blow-dry, a DIY mani-pedi. Dear God, how you need a mani-pedi. By the time the troops swagger in this evening, you'll look like Mrs Brady, perfectly coiffed and groomed, humming a tune while stirring something savory on the stove. Chicken with lemon and capers, you think.

But first there is cleaning to do. You look around, briefly consider Googling a crime scene clean-up service, then shake your head. No, you've got this. You're unstoppable. A few hours without distraction, and you'll have the place back in tip-top shape.

You begin in the kitchen, scouring the sink and countertops until they shine. You open windows, sort mail, dust the china cabinet and breakfront. You spray lemon Pledge throughout the living room and shimmy between coffee and cocktail tables, wielding a dust rag like a ribbon dancer. You vacuum.

Back in the kitchen, you sweep crumbs from the tile floor. There are far too many, so you squint – and see ants. Ants everywhere. You toss the broom aside and start vacuuming. As soon as the ants are sucked away, more re-appear.

No worries, you've got this. A slight detour up to your bedroom office for a Google consult. Cinnamon, you learn, is the answer.

Multitasking, you snatch a basket of laundry and teeter down to the basement, load the washer. You remember that you need to defrost chicken for dinner. By the time you get back to the kitchen, though, the only thing you remember are the ants. You pull cinnamon from the spice rack and sprinkle it in the creases between floor and walls. You head upstairs, pull sheets off beds, douse the toilets with cleaner and Windex the mirrors. You bring the overflowing trashcans downstairs, only to discover the breeze through the open windows has blown cinnamon all over the kitchen floor. The ants seem to like it. You vacuum again and feel ants crawling on your legs.

You go downstairs to deal with the laundry. Someone had a red pen in a pocket. Ink blobs with fine spider-leg projections stain all the light clothing, and the bottom of the washer drum is permanently dyed the color of blood. A few futile squirts of stain spray, then you return upstairs to Google "ink removal". You learn its hopeless, so you shop for new clothes on Amazon.

In the basement, you put over another load – this time you check the pockets – and remember the chicken. But in the kitchen, audacious cinnamon-coated ants are scurrying across the kitchen floor like its open-skate at the ice-rink. So, you forget the chicken and go out to the garage where you sort through a neglected collection of dirty bottles perched on a rusty shelf. You locate ant poison – *Safe for Humans!* – and return to the kitchen. You follow the label instructions, then go outside to escape the fumes and pound the welcome mat.

You vacuum up the ants again, fewer this time. You need to vacuum upstairs, but the vacuum is making funny noises now because the chamber is overstuffed. The thought of cleaning it out roils your gut because it is filled with dust and hair and cinnamon and ants. So, you put the vacuum out in the backyard. You retrieve the dust-buster from the utility closet. Slowly and painfully, you dust-bust the upstairs rugs. You carry the sheets down to the laundry.

You meet your husband in the kitchen. He's picked up your son who is dribbling a basketball on the kitchen floor, unwittingly crushing ants. He says it smells like cinnamon.

Your husband asks what's for dinner. You never did defrost that chicken. You hang your head and glimpse gnarly toenails, still in desperate need of a pedi. You think of how you will need to have a pair of closed-toe shoes *afoot* for your office return tomorrow, then laugh maniacally at your own wit. You sort of want to cry.

Order a pizza, you say.

About the author
Laura Cody is a forensic psychiatrist in New York. Her fiction has appeared or will appear in *Ponder Review, Coffin Bell, Cosmopolitan* (digital edition), *Pussy Magic Heals*, and *Bewildering Stories*. She is currently working with a partner on an adventure series that follows five childhood friends in the aftermath of a global catastrophe.

Busy Bee

June Webber

Honey and lemon

Everyone in the village, except for one, loved Vanessa. Since she and her husband Bill had retired there three years earlier, she had brought new life to the village. She had been elected to the parish council and saved the village school and the bus service. She was a school governor, chair of the W.I., and arranged the flowers in church. When lockdown came, she shopped for the shielding, made scrubs for the hospital and volunteered at the vaccination clinic. Meetings transferred to Zoom, so she spent hours shut away in her study.

Whenever Bill ventured out, which was rare these days, people would remark how kind Vanessa was, and what a difference she had made to the village. "You're a lucky man," they remarked, at which Bill grunted behind his mask.

"Can you do the washing and put the dinner on love?" she called out to Bill one day. "I've got an extra shift at the clinic, and I'll be late back."

Vanessa arrived home to find a suitcase on the bed and piles of shirts and underclothes spread around.

"Where do you think you are going?" she asked. "You know our holiday was cancelled."

"I'm leaving you," he informed her brusquely.

Vanessa's mouth opened wide. "You can't," she gasped. "Where will you go? What will you do without me?"

"All our working lives," Bill began, "we were rushing around and never having much time to relax. I looked forward to retiring to a quiet place in the country, where we could enjoy our life together, going for walks, having a drink in the pub, and sitting in the garden. Instead, you're always out or on a Zoom meeting. You just treat me like a dogsbody to do the shopping and housework, whilst you lord it over the village being a pillar of the community."

"I only wanted to be useful, but if you want me to stay at home more, I expect I could," offered Vanessa grudgingly.

"Too late now," retorted Bill. "Whilst you have been at the clinic or wherever, I have been online to a dating agency and met a lovely widow who likes country walks and pub meals and makes me feel wanted. I'm moving in with her to form a bubble!"

About the author

June Webber writes short stories, flash fiction and poetry, and attends a U3A creative writing group and an online poetry group.

An Unexpected Visitor

Michelle Adams

Breakfast tea from a chipped china tea-cup

The anniversary was always hard. Despite the word conjuring images of joy and celebration, this anniversary was one of sorrow for Emma. Blowing gently to cool the hot tea, Emma took a hesitant sip of her drink, the thin edge of the old china smooth against her lip. Cradling the cup, she closed her eyes and tilted her head upwards towards the warm May sun that made her cheeks feel rosy. The light breeze caressed her skin, carrying with it the promise of summer. Grief wasn't for summer and sunny days. Grief was for winter; for the bitter cold, for harsh grey skies and temperatures that turned your bones to ice; for days when the clouds cried with you and the wind howled its grief too. Five years hadn't eased the pain she felt at losing her mother, though she was learning to live with the constant ache of missing her.

Emma didn't spend much time outdoors; gardening had never been her thing, and the garden was her mother's domain. She had loved the spring, the new growth, the air alive with the sound of nature waking up and new life bursting into being wherever you looked. It had become something of a tradition for Emma to take her morning tea outside on the patio, from her mother's favourite cup. It seemed fitting, the perfect way to remember her. She forced herself to focus on the good times, the happy times, the days of her childhood, the time before her mother became ill. "No good will come of dwelling on the sad times," her mother used to say.

As she sat in the warm garden, Emma found herself remembering the last time that she'd been outside with her mother. They'd sat together on a bench where they could appreciate the late spring blooms and the neatly clipped lawns and hedges. The sweet scent of honeysuckle carried to them across the lawn and mingled with the soft aroma of her mother's lavender perfume.

"What do you think comes next?" her mother had asked tentatively, for they'd avoided the subject that loomed imminently. Her mother waited quietly, giving Emma a moment to compose her answer.

"I don't know," she replied honestly. "Something, I hope. Something." She paused. "Like this. Peaceful." The question had surprised Emma as her mother had always been sceptical about the afterlife, scoffing at notions of heaven and hell. She'd supposed that her mother must finally have been questioning the idea as she came to terms with her mortality. Emma let her gaze sweep across the landscape, the peaceful and picturesque vista perfect for this type of quiet contemplation, for this place. She felt her mother's hand settle across her own, the older woman's skin cool and dry, in contrast to her own soft warmth.

"I'll come back and let you know," she suggested, amusement in the idea evident in her tone and in the crinkles that lined her eyes and mouth.

"And have you scare me silly, seeing your ghost pop out of nowhere!" Emma joined in the joke.

"Don't be daft, love," her mother had replied, suddenly serious, "I'll give you a sign, something only we'd know about." They'd lapsed into silence for a while then, though the air around them filled with birdsong and the distant sound of braying cattle. Movement at the bird table caught Emma's eye, and she gently drew her mother's attention to the new occupant helping itself to the bounty of nuts and seeds. A small red squirrel sat shyly enjoying its breakfast, the evicted blue-tits chattering loudly at its cheek. "That's it!" she'd declared. "I'll visit you as a red squirrel!" Emma laughed at her mother's delight.

"Well, you'll certainly stand out," she said. "We don't see many of them in our village."

"Exactly," her mother had replied, pleased at the idea.

Emma smiled at the memory, so clear even now. As she finished her tea, she became aware of a change in the atmosphere of her garden, an unfamiliar stillness that made her shiver despite the warm day. She looked out across the small space, her gaze settling on the untidy lawn. She gasped, immediate tears welled in her eyes, and her breath caught on the lump that had formed in her throat.

Sat calmly on its hind-legs, watching her with its little head tilted to the side inquisitively, was a small red squirrel, its bushy tail standing up behind it like an exclamation mark. Emma froze, not even daring to breathe too deeply. The squirrel took a few cautious steps towards her – one step, then two more. Time seemed to stop as Emma watched, waiting to see what the little creature did next. A car door slammed in the distance, and the collie at No.2 barked furiously. In an instant, the magic that held them both in place vanished. Emma started and the squirrel, quick and nimble, scurried away through the garden hedge.

Emma took a steadying breath and forced her shaking hands to still. Did she dare believe what she had seen? Could it be? A soothing blanket of calm enveloped her, and she suddenly felt a lightness she hadn't realised had been missing. She inhaled deeply and caught the scent of honeysuckle and then lavender, fading quickly. Maybe, she thought. Just maybe.

About the author

Michelle Adams lives on Anglesey, North Wales. Since turning 40 a few years ago, she has returned to study and is currently a student with The Open University, studying towards a BA in Arts & Humanities (English Language & Creative Writing).

JUNE

All of the stories published on CaféLit *in June 2021 were good. But the ones featured here really shine out.*

Nick Young's Granna *is short and poignant as two generations connect over the divide.*

S. Nadja Zajdman charms us in Setting the Template *with a story of sibling support.*

Billie Pritchett's A Woman, Her Cow and Her Hen *is succinct, fable-like and charming as a woman learns that she shouldn't really be fixing what isn't broken.*

Amy B. Moreno in just a few lines warns about how we should take care of what we gift to children.

Nickel *is one of Jim Bates' Element stories. We can again enjoy here Jim's rich story-teller voice.*

As ever Lynn Clement gets to the heart of the matter in The People. *There is some lovely evocation of a seaside place waking up again here. And we are intrigued. What exactly is the narrator's problem? What happens next seems to help or does it?*

About the editor

Gill James, writer, editor and creative writing lecturer.

www.gilljameswriter.com/

Granna

Nick Young

Black coffee sweetened with sugar

She couldn't know — how could she?

She was but five, so she couldn't know that the ancient figure across the room was anything but stooped by the weight of time. She couldn't know that once that woman with brittle skin etched by life's toil was as full of joy as she, reveling in the summer sun as she ran, laughing, through the dazzling wildflowers sprinkled up the slope of the low hillside that rose toward a patch of thick timber behind the faded brick farmhouse. How could she know that as a schoolgirl the old one was bright, full of curiosity about the world and thirsty as a sponge for knowledge? Or that in her teenage years, she kept a secret diary, confiding in its deckled pages the thrill of kissing a boy for the first time and her dreams of going to a college in the ivied East and living in a city with soaring buildings of dizzying heights. She couldn't know how those yearnings were crushed away to dust by parents who put no stock in a girl having "them notions", prodding her relentlessly so that she finally surrendered, exhausted, abandoned her books and fell in with a fast crowd, living loose, for the thrill of the moment, roiling convention, flouting rectitude. How could she know that the woman before her with lank gray hair and a stolid thickness about her once had a pin-up's face and a body that was all tightness and curves, driving men to frenzies of passion and jealousy sometimes settled with fists or a knife. She could not know about the barroom nights that ended, panting, in a back seat or a shabby room in a rundown motel on the far side of the railroad tracks. And she could not know how the people of the town whispered cruelly behind the woman's back, even as she strove to pull free of wantonness, refashion her life and let the past slip into the distance of memory.

No, she didn't know -- how could she?

What she did know was that this is old soul in the faded cornflower-blue shift who shuffled so slowly, hardly lifting her worn slippers as she moved, would never fail to bring her favorite teddy, to see them both safely tucked within the cocoon of blankets infused with the faint scent of cedar as the evening drew down. And she knew this woman would bend low to stroke her hair with tremulous hand, place a gentle kiss upon her forehead, smile and whisper that the night would hold no terrors and the morning would come with warm sunshine and bright birdsong.

About the author

Nick Young is a retired award-winning CBS News Correspondent. His writing has appeared in *The Nonconformist* magazine, the *San Antonio Review, Samjoko Magazine, Short Story Town, Danse Macabre Magazine, Pigeon Review,* the *Green Silk Journal, Typeslash Review, The Potato Soup Journal, 50-Word Stories, Sein und Werden, Of Rust and Glass, Little Death Lit, Flyover Magazine, Sandpiper, Fiery Scribe Review, The Chamber Magazine* and Vols. I and II of the *Writer Shed Stories* anthologies.

Setting the Template

S. Nadja Zajdman

Milk and cookies

From the age of three, until I became eligible for kindergarten, I was enrolled at Mary Beetles, a pre-school in the days before daycare programs. It was run by Miss Mary Beetles, a single and independent woman then referred to as a spinster. Her surname was spelled like the name of the insect, before a British pop group changed it.

On stage at a Christmas recital, I wore a pink dress with short puffed sleeves. A petticoat puffed up my short skirt, and a band of fake pink rose petals decorated my thick and dark hair. I was not yet self-conscious about my thick and heavy thighs, though I was acutely aware of the clunky, ankle-length orthopedic shoes that encased my wide, flat and weak feet. I shook cymbals and tapped a tambourine. I had natural rhythm, effortlessly kept the beat, and felt perfectly comfortable on what was the first of many stages I would find myself on in years to come.

The only light in the darkness of the hall emanated from the equipment of the hired photographer taking the pictures that were going to be sold to our parents once they were developed. The one disruption came from the back of the hall. A toddler seated on his mother's lap stretched for a better view of the stage, and suddenly erupted into a high-pitched scream.

"Dat's my shister! Dat's my shister!" He broke out of his mother's arms, dropped to the floor, tore up the centre aisle, and tried to hoist himself onto the stage. Caught between footlights, with one chubby thigh on the boards, and straining to lift his diaper-covered bottom, my baby brother raised his luminous, blueberry-hued eyes and beamed his baby-toothed grin at me.

"Shashi! Shashi!" Mikey called out the nickname he had given me. He seemed confused when I didn't dash over to help him, and surprised by the uncharacteristic scowl on my face. Clearly, he couldn't fathom why I wasn't as thrilled to see him as he was to see me.

Instinctively, I grasped the concept and convention of The Fourth Wall, and my adorable and adoring brother was breaking it! In this, my first crisis, I proved a trouper, stoically soldiering on while never missing a beat on my tambourine.

While the audience rocked with laughter, a policeman who had been standing guard at the back door rushed to the bottom of the stage, scooped Mikey into his arms, and carried him away.

"But she's my shister!" Mikey implored the policeman. Could the cop not comprehend the sacredness of the sibling bond? Oblivious to the giggles of the onlookers, patiently, pointedly, Mikey attempted to explain. "My SHISTER!"

The policeman merely smiled, and brought Mikey to the back of the hall.

Our recital proceeded without further incident. By the time it was over, the cop and the toddler had bonded. Mikey was leaning back, relaxed in the policeman's arms, with the policeman's oversized hat sliding down and masking the top half of his head.

Denied access to the main stage, the beguiling tyke created his own. While the cop held Mikey, Mikey's sweet and sunny nature held the cop enthralled.

In years to come, the world became my brother's stage. There were no barriers that could not be broken, no obstacles that could not be overcome, nor any arbitrary rules that could not be bent nor circumvented. Michael's irrepressible spirit and irresistible charm remain intact. So does his attachment to me.

About the author

S. Nadja Zajdman is a Canadian author. Her fiction and non-fiction writing has been featured in newspapers, magazines, literary journals and anthologies across North America, in the UK, Australia and New Zealand. With *Hobart Books* in Oxford, Zajdman published the memoir *I Want You To Be Free*. With *Bridge House Publishing*, she published the story collection *The Memory Keeper*. Scheduled for publication is Zajdman's debut novel *The More Loving One*, as well as a second story collection, *Bent Branches*. In 2021, Zajdman received an award from The Society of Authors Foundation in London.

A Woman, Her Cow and Her Hen

Billie Pritchett

Raw milk

A woman had a hen that laid an egg every morning. Every weekend the woman sold all the eggs at the market. The eggs were so good, of such fine quality, that the woman always made a high profit.

One day, she figured if she gave her hen more barley, the hen would produce twice the eggs. But after she gave the hen the extra barley, the hen got so fat she stopped producing eggs altogether. That was the end of the woman's egg-selling business.

She was grateful, though, she still had her cow. She went to the cow, grabbed the udders, and started squirting the milk into the pail. Then, bouncing her knees, making the change jingle in her pockets, she said to herself, "It's no good messing with a good thing, is it?"

About the author

Billie Pritchett is an assistant professor of English at Kyungnam University in Masan, Korea. He has an MFA in Creative Writing from Murray State University. His work is forthcoming in *Concho River Review, Delmarva Review, Drunk Monkeys,* and *Pensive.*

Product Review

Amy B. Moreno

A single shot espresso

Product Review: "Jungle Fun" Toddler Drum Kit – (with "real clang" cymbal set).

Loud, obnoxious, and with no "off" button, this toddler drum kit is bright neon in both colour and volume.

Perfect gift to the toddler of a parent you hate. Tantrums guaranteed (and not from the 2-year-old).

10/10 value for money. Would recommend!

About the author

Amy B. Moreno writes poetry and fiction for adults and children, in English, Scots, and Spanish, including multilingual pieces. Her new bilingual picture book, *A Billion Balloons of Questions* is to be published by *Floris* in June 2022.

Nickel

Jim Bates

Black coffee

I'll be the first to admit that I should probably do a better job staying in touch with my siblings. I'm the oldest after all, and Mom instilled in me from an early age that I should, as she put it many, many times while we were growing up, "Always watch out for your brothers and sisters. They look up to you, you know."

Well, maybe in Mom's world they did, but in real life there was not even the faintest pretense of looking up. We fought most of the time and didn't have a lot of love lost between us. Something that has mitigated only slightly over time. So, I might be excused when it comes to staying in better touch with them.

But my littlest brother, Russ, well, there was something there. We are close. It's a bond that's stayed with us our entire lives. Maybe it's because I once almost killed him.

Not on purpose, of course, but I take full responsibility for what happened. That summer I was eight and Russ was a two-year-old bundle of energy getting into everything and making life challenging for my mom and dad and a pain in the ass for the rest of us.

"Make sure you watch out for little Russ," she told me time and time again.

"Right, Mom," I said, feeling I should snap a salute. I was already looking after six-year-old Allie, five-year-old Jarvis and three-year-old Gwen. What was one more?

But it was summertime and I was a kid. When was I supposed to have any fun? At least I had my coin collection. I'd been collecting nickels ever since I'd gotten a collecting book from my uncle that previous Christmas. It was blue and had slots for nickels that you'd fill. It was fun. I'd go to the bank with my hard-earned money made from shoveling our neighbor's sidewalk during the winter or mowing their lawn during the summer, hand over two dollars, and bingo! I'd come home with a roll of forty nickels to add to my collection.

I usually kept it hidden under the mattress of my bed, but on that day, I must have inadvertently left it out.

I heard Mom screaming all the way from the backyard where I was playing on the swing set with Allie and Jarvis and Gwen. "My, god! Russ ate the coins!"

Oh, oh. I knew right away what she was getting at. I wanted to run away, but made myself run inside instead.

I burst into the kitchen." What's up?"

Mom slapped me on the back of the head. "Don't

play 'what's up?' with me, young man. Why weren't you watching your brother?" She pointed at Russ, sitting on the kitchen floor, grinning and patting his stomach. He looked fine to me. "Russ swallowed your coins," Mom repeated.

I made a snap decision not to argue with her about he was supposed to have been taking a nap in their bedroom. He must have gotten up and started wandering around the house. How was I supposed to know? But right now didn't seem like the right time to debate the issue.

Instead, I went for conciliatory. "Geez, Mom. I'm sorry," I told her. I really was. I didn't mind my little brother all that much. In general, he was pretty easy to take care of. He'd apparently toddled into the kitchen grasping a handful of my coins. Mom had pried them out of his fat fingers and assumed the worst; that he'd eaten some. That's when I'd heard her screams.

I knelt down, smiled, and said, "Hi, buddy." He seemed fine to me. He was barefoot, wearing a pair of red shorts and a white tee-shirt with Bugs Bunny on it. He grinned at me and sputtered something. Then he frowned and started coughing. Then he threw up.

Mom picked him up and ran of the kitchen yelling over her shoulder, "You take care of the kids. I'm taking him to the hospital." She gave me a withering look. "Don't screw up!"

I was horrified at what I'd done and actually felt like I was going to throw up. But I didn't. Instead, I watched as she loaded Russ into the baby seat of the old Plymouth and pealed out of the driveway. I ran back to the swing set where my brother and sisters were still playing and herded them inside. None of them had any idea of the tragedy that had just occurred with Russ, but I certainly did. I kid you not, the two hours between when Mom left and when she came home were the longest of my life. I thought for sure he'd die. And if he died, I thought for sure I'd go to jail, at least, if not prison. I got my siblings playing in the living room while I sat glued to the front window. Along with watching my brother and sisters, of course.

When Mom pulled into the driveway and carried Russ inside, I started crying. I'd never been so happy in my life. I wasn't going to jail!! Oh, yeah, I was happy he was still alive, too.

Mom set Russ down at the kitchen table with a bowl of ice cream. "It's for his throat," she told me. "They had to pump his stomach."

She gave me a bowl as well and sat down with me and Russ. "I know it's hard," she told me, mussing up my hair. "Thank you." I have to say, that ice cream tasted good on my throat, too.

The image of my brother lying on a table in the hospital with a thick rubber hose jammed down his throat while someone pumped a bellows of some sort has stayed with me my entire life, even though I'm pretty sure it was less invasive. Pretty sure. Honestly, I never asked.

I paid special attention to Russ from then. Probably initially from guilt, because, like Mom continued to remind me, my little brother easily could have died. But then I got so I liked him. He had a good sense of humor and was pretty funny. He had a pleasant disposition and was easy to be around. I did things with him like play catch, and when he was older, I taught him to ride a bike. He liked to read and so did I.

So, it didn't turn out too bad. In fact, a few years after the coin incident we started collecting stamps together. They were a lot safer than coins, and Mom was all for it.

"Eat as many as you want," I'd tell him, sitting at the kitchen table sorting out a new bundle of stamps. We'd laugh.

But the day of the coins will always live on in our family. When Russ tells the story, he always makes sure to add, "To be honest, they didn't taste too bad," he tells anyone who will listen. "Kind of metallic, though. If you know what I mean."

Sometimes, I'm the only one who laughs at his joke. Maybe people are getting tired of it. After all, it happened twenty-eight years ago. Or, maybe it's from a long-held sense of relief that things turned out okay that day when he swallowed those nickels.

All I know is that he's alive and we get along great and that's what matters. Plus, no matter what anyone says, I still think he's kind of funny.

About the author

Jim lives in a small town twenty miles west of Minneapolis, Minnesota. His stories and poems have appeared in over three hundred online and print publications. *Short Stuff*, a collection of drabbles and flash fiction, was published in July 2021, by *Chapeltown Books*. Additional stories can be found on his blog:
www.theviewfromlonglake.wordpress.com.

The People

Lynn Clement

Black coffee

The people are coming back, now the winter has gone. Only in dribs and drabs but its noticeable. The noise is greater.

I enjoyed the sometimes stillness and the almost silence. Just the shushing of the waves upon the rocks. I even enjoyed the storms, as the sand battered the windows like bullets and the lights flickered, threatening to give up. I had my candles at the ready. I would have enjoyed that too. Just me and the wind, the sea, and the dark.

But now the people are back.

I'll go out later, in the evening. They won't be on the beach then. They'll all be fair-weatherers.

The sea is even nicer in the dusk, with its shadows of charcoal and grey. The smell of the seaweed clings to the air and the salty tang works its way into the corners of my mouth. I'll wear my clogs and kick them off so that the gritty sand can play in between my toes, whilst I sit and listen to the shush of the merciful waves.

I've been doing that all winter. Sometimes it's been bitter. But I did it. It made me feel alive. That's why I'm here. To feel alive.

To feel.

There's one of them.

A fair-weatherer. Huge bag of stuff. Windbreak, towels, ball, picnic, radio. Plastic bags that will blow on the breeze and end up at the bottom of the Mariana Trench. Why can't they leave us alone? Leave me alone.

I need to be alone.

A child is laughing outside my window. So, I shut it and go into my kitchen at the back of the house where I can't see them.

The letter is on the kitchen table, where I'd flung it.

The coffee mug is warm, and I wrap my hands around it, staring at the letter. Six months is all it took. Twenty-eight or so weeks to un-ravel the threads of my life.

Again.

To tell me the hospital has no case to answer.

There is a pain like a dagger-blow in my chest. I always feel that now. The letter has just reminded me to keep on feeling it, and not to let the sand and the sea heal it too much, or too soon.

Tapping on the window rouses me. I think I'd fallen asleep. Is it another storm? Surely not, the sky was bright blue this morning. The sun is shining into my yellow kitchen making me blink.

The tap again. It's not loud, soft like a… child's.

It is a child.

She looks six years old. She has curly blonde hair. She's covering her eyes with her little hand so that she can peer into my window. I can't see the colour of her eyes. I think they'll be blue. Huge blue eyes, with big black dots in the middle, and a pink rosebud mouth that will curl up at the corners. I wonder if her name is Ellie too.

She waves as I stare at her, and my heart races.

"Hello!" shouts a voice. Not the child. It's a man. "Hello, sorry to disturb you but could we have our ball back? It's gone into your garden."

I close my eyes and have a battle with myself. Shall I, or shan't I?

I wonder if she does have blue eyes.

The warmth feels good on my face as I open the door to retrieve the little girl's ball.

About the author

Lynn is a regular writer for *CaféLit*. She has recently worked with CaféLit author, Allison Symes, on the final edit of her first flash fiction collection, *The City of Stories*. Lynn is a member of Basingstoke group, Writers inc. Lynn now has a Facebook page:
www.facebook.com/lynnclementauthor

JULY

July's stories are a mixed bag.

Odd Todd *is paired with an unusual choice of drink. Absinthe became fashionable among artists in 19th century Paris, producing hallucinations and destroying minds. Todd's story is a vivid journey into the mind of a dangerous person, someone who battles to control his own vile thoughts. Where is the line between truth and hallucinations?*

Trial by Furniture, A Cautionary Tale *uses the bare minimum of words to convey both the petty irritations of living with a partner – "put your drink on the glass, not on the wood" – and the numbing sense of loss that follows the disappearance of that partner.*

Hey Ma, Look at Me *reads like a painful, personal memoir – "that spastic fat kid who can't even get herself up and down the ladder." It weaves the narrator's present and past, together with her mother's past, into a missive of gratitude for the force of mother love.*

All-Seeing Izabella *at first appears to be a straightforward description of a trip to the seaside, written by a grumpy, over-protective older sister. "So, here we were on a frigid weekend to see if a mechanical doll in its little Perspex booth could help Marie move on." Unexpected news on the pier confounds both their expectations.*

About the editor

Madeleine McDonald writes flash fiction, radio stories and romance novels. Her work has appeared in *Mslexia* and *The London Reader,* among other journals.

Odd Todd

Sandra Nguyen

Absinthe

Todd glanced at the ceiling. He had come to recognize the pair of dark eyes that stared at him, and the vile thoughts behind them. Last time he saw those eyes, they spoke to him, telling him to hurt Jim, his neighbor. The image of him holding the knife, forcing the sharp blade onto Jim's arm, and slicing it open, made him crumble on the inside. Todd never forgave himself for what he did. He never wanted to hurt Jim, or anyone, but the eyes would not leave him alone until he did what it asked for. After that incident Todd decided he needed help. He was a danger to others.

Todd blamed the car accident, in which he sustained a brain injury. He started seeing things, and hearing things, that no one in his surrounding could see or hear. His life spiraled quickly downhill, and soon he earned the nickname Odd Todd when he told people he could see the shadow people, and that they constantly whispered to him. The shadow people reminded him of humanoid figures. Sometimes he could catch a glimpse of them out of the corner of his eyes. But most often, he only saw their eyes. Those things thrived on human suffering. They could attach themselves onto a vulnerable person, like a bloodsucking leech, and fed on their life energy. They would whisper into your ears – forcing you to do things against your will, planting seeds of lies and deception, casting shadows of despair, until you become crippled from the inside and out. They want to keep you in the dark and afraid.

This place was like a feast buffet for the shadow people and there was nothing Todd could do about it. He had his own battle, and was struggling losing the one lurking in the ceiling. All he could do was watch his peers slowly deteriorating as their life force diminished, losing their mind, and become a living puppet. Todd looked at Miss Camilla, the young nurse he had come to like. He pressed himself against the wall, both hands on his head, trying to fight off the vile thought. He knew what the eyes wanted him to do. It painted him a very vivid and repulsive vision. A vision in which he could feel his strong hands gripping around Camilla's neck, draining her life essence as she struggled to breathe when he closed off her air pipe. Camilla turned around and gazed at him, her fingers nervously fumbling the cross-necklace, sensing his disturbing thought. Ashamed and angry at the thought of hurting Camilla, Todd made sure he was out of her sight.

Big Danny entered the common room with a newcomer. Holly Hager was her name. She seemed so small standing next to him. She let Big Danny lead the way and seated her in the chair. Todd noticed she did not take her eyes off the ceiling, shaking her head in protest, as if someone forced her to do something against her will. He asked Big Danny for a piece of paper and some crayons, and began drawing, using only black crayon to draw the eyes and the rest of the humanoid figure. He walked over to Holly when he finished the drawing. She didn't seem to pay him any attention, her eyes still locked on the ceiling. He put his drawing on the table and gently pushed the box of crayons closer to her. Holly stared at him, then picked out a single black crayon. She flipped the paper and started off with few soft streaks, then quickly sped up the pace. His eyes widened when he saw Jim in the drawing, fending off Todd from piercing his chest with a kitchen knife. Holly even drew the dark eyes next to him, whispering in his ears. She pointed to the ceiling and then pointed to the dark eyes in the drawing. Todd was aghast at the accuracy of the drawing, but how did she know?

Miss Katie came into the room to gather her horde for recreational therapy class. It was Todd's favorite activity. He watched Holly, with a mixture of amusement and jealousy, smearing black crayon all over the white paper. He wished he had half of her talent. The drawing depicted Nellie Lindh surrounded by three pairs of dark eyes. Todd traced his finger along the painted tears that rolled down Nelly's cheek. He turned his head and caught Nelly smiling at him, and just like in the drawing, she was surrounded by three pairs of dark eyes. Holly pointed at the clock in the drawing, ten o'clock it said, and then counted down with her fingers – five, four, three, two, one. Todd wasn't sure what Holly tried to tell him, but it left him helpless and horrified. After class he turned in Holly's drawing to Miss Katie. She was bewildered when he told her that they needed to keep an eye on Nellie at ten o'clock tonight.

That night, Todd dreaded falling asleep. He was afraid that if he fell asleep he wouldn't see Nellie again. Sweet Nellie who wouldn't hurt a fly. He listened impatiently for any sign of chaos, and then it happened. Someone called "code blue", followed by footsteps and voices, but these did not belong to the night staff. He strained his ears to catch a sound, but he found himself sinking deeper and deeper in the abyss. The sleep medication was kicking in.

The following day Todd was scheduled to see his therapist Mr Bentzen. In his hand he held Holly's drawing.

"Todd, I want to talk about the drawing you made in Miss Katie's class," Mr Bentzen started.

"It's not my drawing," Todd replied. "Holly drew it."

"Who's Holly?" Mr Bentzen wondered. Todd started laughing hysterically. Was Mr Bentzen blind? Holly sat next to him.

"Holly Hager, of course. There's only one Holly in this room," Todd answered.

Mr Bentzen froze at the mentioning of Holly Hager. He recalled the name vividly. Holly was one of his patients. She was a very special patient, didn't talk much, but used drawing as a mean of communication. Mr Bentzen carefully examined the drawing again. How did he miss it? The drawing had Holly's signature all over it. She always drew with black crayon. And those eyes she drew, they always made his skin crawl whenever he looked at them. His eyes caught something at the bottom left corner – Holly's signature, H.H. It was barely visible, but it was there. Mr Bentzen scratched his head. He knew Todd was not artistic, but Miss Katie had insisted it was Todd who made the drawing in her class. He debated with himself, whether or not, he should tell Todd that Holly Hager had passed away five years ago.

"Todd, Miss Hager is no longer with us," Mr Bentzen decided it was best for Todd to hear the truth.

"I know," Todd answered. "And neither is Nellie."

Mr Bentzen felt a sudden chill surrounding him. He jotted down in his notes "Dr Pinsky", and quickly wrapped up the conversation. He thought perhaps Dr Pinsky could adjust Todd's medication, since his hallucinations had worsened the past few days.

Before leaving the unit, Mr Bentzen made a call to the hospital and asked for Nellie Lindh. His face had turned white as he listened to the voice on the other side of the telephone line.

"Poor Mr Bentzen, he just found out that Nellie is dead," Holly said.

"Should we tell him that he has one of those leeches following him?" Nellie wondered.

"Nah, he wouldn't believe us," Todd said.

About the author

Sandra Nguyen was born in Vietnam and raised in Sweden. She writes short stories and poetry. Her work has been featured in anthologies as well as in online publications. She lives and writes in Sweden. You can follow her writing journey here: www.thetopazjournal.com/

Trial by Furniture, a Cautionary Tale

Franci Hepburn

Pomegranate juice

I bought an Arthur G leather couch for the Mid-century in Claremont we moved into. I added the Danish glass and wood coffee table, vintage, and the Marcel Breuer Ceska chairs, original. We drank tea in the morning from Marc Newson (for Noritake) and Pinot Noir from Riedel at sunset.

I kept warning: don't sit on the chair with your wet bathers, and I was right, wasn't I? The rattan on the seat split, only suitable for the verge collection now. I also said: don't sit on the same spot every day. Your jeans will stain the coach, please work in the study or in a bedroom, for goodness sakes; the house has six bedrooms and: put your drink on the glass, not on the wood, it makes white rings.

Now the seat is not only hollow on one side, lopsided like a badly risen bread. It also has a blue stain in the shape of a charging mountain goat, meeting me every morning when I open the curtains. But alone in the house, day after day, the hollowed-out bread, the charging goat, the circles like white-rimmed glasses on the coffee table staring at me accusingly. Highlighting my solitude.

About the author

Franci Hepburn is an artist and writer who has written manuscripts and regularly enters short stories into competitions. She enjoys observing people and creating characters in all forms. Franci teaches Art at a secondary school in Perth Hills, where she lives. Franci writes in English, her second language.

Hey Ma, Look at Me

S. Nadja Zajdman

Lemonade

During the first week of September I swim in my neighbourhood's outdoor community pool. The day camps have closed, and the children have returned to school. With the children gone and a softer sun beaming on the water and on me, I feel as if I'm vacationing at a resort. There is no ocean on the horizon and there are no waving palm trees, but strangely enough there are gulls wheeling in the clear blue sky. On the outlying lawn butterflies flit onto fuzzy-headed purple clover, bumble bees drone in the background, and the first yellow leaves dive into the water and land at the bottom of the competition-sized pool. I can see them clearly as I propel myself through water warmer than the air, which has a nip in it. I am wearing prescription goggles, which enables me to open my eyes and see underwater as clearly as I did when I was a five-year-old learning to swim.

I didn't want to learn. My mother insisted upon it. The first six months of swimming lessons were an ordeal. By bus, in the dead of winter, even in blizzards. my mother and I would drag ourselves to the YMYWHA. It took the good part of half an hour to relieve myself of the layers of clothing and the heavy coat and scarf and hat and boots I was bundled in, in order to get into my bathing suit. A hard plastic cap had to be stretched and fitted over my heavy braids, which placed unremitting pressure upon my skull. When I whined about the effort involved my mother would snap, "You are going to learn. One day, you will thank me."

It was when I squeezed into the bathing suit and bathing cap that the worst part loomed. I had to enter the pool area and climb down a ladder into the water. I was awkward and fat. My swim mates mocked me. The saving grace was our teacher, Paul Rosenthal. I remember his name, and I shall always remember him. He was a German Jew, a refugee from The Third Reich. I don't know when nor how he escaped, but Paul Rosenthal's survival and entry into my existence set me on a course that saved the quality of my life.

By the time I was placed into my swim teacher's paw-like palms, he must've been in his forties. He was muscular and handsome, with a tenderness that belied his physical bulk. Paul – if memory serves, we called him Paul, not Mr Rosenthal – paid extra attention and took special care of me. He would stand halfway between one end of the lane and the other and coax, "Just this far, Sharon. Come, come. Swim to me only this far. You can do it. I know you can do it." As I frantically paddled towards Paul, he would surreptitiously back up until he reached the end of the lane. Then he would scoop me into his warm, strong arms and exult, "Look Sharon! Look behind you!" I gasped with surprise and growing confidence when I realized how far I had come. "You see! You swam all the way across the pool!" By spring I had become the star of the class, bouncing on the diving board and shouting across the water, to the outlying stands, "Hey Ma! Look at me!"

During the winter I learned to swim, my mother was going through anguish of her own. Mum had never learned to swim. When she was seven years old, her father threw her into a local stream in a practical application of the adage that what doesn't sink, will survive. As Mum started to drown her father's sister fished her out of the water and turned on her brother, cursing him with invectives that were a Polish equivalent of "What were you thinking?!" This violent form of baptism left Mum with a lifelong fear of water. Yet seven years later she would wade through the slime and rat-infested sewers of Warsaw, escaping its infamous Ghetto. For Mum, the ability to swim was equated with survival.

While keeping vigil in the spectator stand of the pool area at the Y, Mum silently endured the nastiness of the other mothers as they watched me struggling to climb up and down the ladder. My classmates' mothers were as cruel as they were. Ironically, or not, the most vicious of the lot was an obese woman by the name of Mrs Shulman. All winter Mum cringed as Mrs Shulman smirked and scoffed at "that spastic fat kid who can't even get herself up and down the ladder. She has no business being here. Why does her mother bother to bring her?!" It was only in spring, when I called out triumphantly from the diving board and Mum acknowledged me with a curt nod, that Mrs Shulman realized who had been listening to her rants. She may have become embarrassed, if she was capable of embarrassment, but from then on Mrs Shulman bit her virulent tongue. Mum maintained her silence and her dignity, looking beyond the prattling, unaccented women and onto the water, not at me, but at the fellow survivor and refugee who had done for her daughter what she could not. My swim teacher caught the sadness in her haunted eyes and acknowledged Mum's mute gratitude with a slow smile and quiet pride.

Swimming was, and continues to be my salvation. In the years to come I would swim my way through massive weight loss and massive personal loss. From my teenage years on, when my parents moved us into an apartment building with both an indoor and outdoor pool, I rarely lived swimming pool-less. In the years to come, I would coax my mother into the water and support her weightless body so that she could lean back, let go, and experience what it feels like to trust, float and surrender. On seaside vacations Mum would grip my hands while edging sideways into the ocean, in a valiant attempt to conquer her fear of water. She chattered in order to distract herself, and when a wave rose up and slapped her open mouth I laughed, so that she might laugh, too. Wet, refreshed, and worn out by the challenge she had set for herself, Mum would declare, "That's enough!" and retreat to the shore. As the tide ebbed and the sun set she sat in the sand gazing, in fascination, as a group of gulls gathered together, seemingly by appointment, and stood at the edge of the water, patiently waiting, we decided, "For Daddy to bring them home."

My mother is gone now. I plunge into the water while dying yellow leaves drop to the bottom of the community pool and lie still there. As I push and propel, my eyes open and my vision restored, I marvel at how it's possible to feel so fortunate, so grateful, and so intensely lonely, all at the same time. Hey Ma, look at me. I'm still swimming. Thank you.

About the author

S. Nadja Zajdman is a Canadian author. Her fiction and non-fiction writing has been featured in newspapers, magazines, literary journals and anthologies across North America, in the UK, Australia and New Zealand. With *Hobart Books* in Oxford, Zajdman published the memoir *I Want You To Be Free*. With *Bridge House Publishing*, she published the story collection *The Memory Keeper*. Scheduled for publication is Zajdman's debut novel *The More Loving One*, as well as a second story collection, *Bent Branches*. In 2021, Zajdman received an award from The Society of Authors Foundation in London.

All-Seeing Izabella

Yvonne Lang

Herbal tea

There was a salty sea breeze stinging my cheeks as I trudged down the old wooden pier. I'm sacrificing another weekend to support my continuous victim sister, Marie. It's out of season, everything shut down for winter and no-one else is around. A freezing cold beach and closed arcade didn't appeal to anyone else apparently. We weren't here for fun though.

Marie's partner had gone missing almost four months ago. The police had no leads. He had simply vanished. I didn't miss him; I knew my sister was better off without the asshole. The police didn't seem to be searching that hard for him. He was a grown man with a checkered past and no signs of foul play – he wasn't high on their priority list, for which I was glad. I had hated her dating him, was distraught when he moved in with her but knew I couldn't intervene. I had fixed anything that ever went wrong with my sister's life. I took the role of older sister very seriously after we lost our parents and looked out for her. Perhaps too much. The first significant choice she had ever made alone was to date that loser.

His disappearance should have been a chance for her to get her life back on track, but she was devastated. She had no idea if she had been dumped or if he had been a victim. The uncertainty drove her mad and when the police could provide no answers, she started turning to more unusual sources. Ever the supportive sister, and to make sure she wasn't ripped off in her fragile state by some charlatan, I traipsed round with her visiting psychics and mediums. All spouted tosh and none agreed with each other.

Then someone from one of my sister's online support groups had mentioned a fortune teller doll that seemed to know things that were impossible to know. It was giving grieving people answers no-one else had been able to provide.

So, here we were, on a frigid weekend to see if a mechanical doll in its little Perspex booth could help Marie move on. We found the booth; her name was emblazoned on a brass plaque above her – Izabella. Everything else in the arcade looked old, faded. Yet Izabella's face still looked brand new, serene, her blue silk outfit pristine. Something about her gave me the creeps.

Marie's eyes glistened as she approached, the pound coin already in her hand. She pushed it into the slot and waited expectantly. There was a whirring of gears as the doll creaked to life and aged bulbs flashed behind her. The pale white hands moved awkwardly over the cheap looking crystal ball and an automated voice asked, "What answers do you seek?"

Marie told her tearfully. There was more whirring and then the lights faded as the doll stilled. A slip of pale-yellow paper popped out from the machine. Marie snatched at it, but her face fell as she read. She screwed up the paper, tossed it to the floor and stormed off – obviously another dead end.

Curious, I picked up the paper and unfurled it.

"Your sister made sure he was removed from your life for your own good."

I stared, slack jawed at the doll.

"You grass," I said softly.

How did it know? If it knew it was for her own good why throw me under the bus? Maybe that was why Izabella had left out the word "murder" since she knew my motives were pure. Small mercies.

About the author

Yvonne's work has featured in a range of publications, from *Your Cat* and *Northern Life* to *Siren's Call* and *Schlock*. Her stories have appeared in online publications including *Café Lit Magazine* and *The Secret Attic*, with her flash fiction featuring on *Horror Tree*, *The Daily Drabble*, *101 Words* and *Paragraph Planet*. Her debut novella was published by *Demain* as part of the *Short Sharp Shock* Series. She resides in Yorkshire with her partner and a cat who does not respect personal space.

www.yvonnelang.co.uk

AUGUST

I wanted a mixture of length and mood of stories for my pick.

The Stories He Tells You *was deeply moving, shows Alzheimer's well, and it was good to have the viewpoint of the person with it, rather than from family. This story is lovely and sad – not an easy balance to get right – and has a powerful ending.*

For Marmalade, *I have a confession. June Webber is a dear Swanwick friend; she read the story on one of our* Zoom *meetings, and guess who encouraged her to send it in to* CaféLit*?! I was pleased she did. I would have chosen this quirky, humorous tale anyway as I liked how the story packs a lot into few words, for its amusing conclusion, and its identifiable lead character in Annie.*

For A Scratch For An Itch, *the title immediately intrigued me. I also have a soft spot for all-dialogue stories and this one is done well. Loved the ending but must admit to wanting her to give her cheating spouse the boot. Again identifiable characters (which is even more remarkable when you consider they're not named). This tale again packs a lot into a few words.*

About the editor

Allison Symes, who loves quirky fiction, is published by *Chapeltown Books, CaféLit*, and *Bridge House Publishing*. Her flash fiction collections, *From Light to Dark and Back Again* and *Tripping the Flash Fantastic,* are available in Kindle and paperback. She writes weekly for online magazine, *Chandler's Ford Today,* on topics of interest to writers.

Allison also gives workshops on flash fiction on *Zoom* and in person where possible. She is a member of the *Society of Authors* and the *Association of Christian Writers.*

The Stories He Tells You

Michelle Adams

Tea, just how you like it

You're reading this because you didn't recognise the man that gave it to you. That dear, sweet man that visits you every day, who brings you flowers, makes your cup of tea just how you like it and who looks at you with such sadness in his eyes, is your husband, and you've been married for over forty years. His name is James, and you have three children together, Matthew, Katy and Lucy.

You don't remember him because you have an illness, a horrible, horrible illness that is stealing your memories. You wrote this letter shortly after the doctors told you what to expect – ready for this day that you prayed would never come.

You must be very confused and very scared. But NEVER be scared of James – that man would die before he ever hurt you.

It was hard to hear the news you had been dreading. When you first went to the GP, you'd hoped he say that it was just old age creeping up or that it was stress from James' retirement (as much as you love him, it was a little tricky getting used to him being home all day!). Dr Porter was coming up for retirement himself, and in the past, had been a little dismissive of what he called "ladies' problems". An old fashioned gentleman with old fashioned views, you'd expected that he'd wave away your concerns as he had in the past. But that wrinkled old face had frowned, and he'd pulled his chair closer and asked questions, ones that even now you can't quite remember, that linger on the edges of your memory, that evaporate into nothing whenever you try and focus on them. Driving home that day was a blur; you couldn't remember leaving the surgery or even the journey. James found you sitting on the driveway, the engine of your little yellow mini still running, just staring at nothing. You hadn't told him how much it was bothering you, those minor innocuous symptoms he'd made light of, that on their own were nothing more than silly little idiosyncrasies, funny little habits. Some had always been part of your personality, like mixing up words – always calling the dishwasher the washing machine or the oven the sink. But before, those little foibles had been a product of a distracted mind, not a sick one. And in the end, those little things, when put together, turned out to be quite a big thing. Alzheimer's. A funny-sounding word for something that isn't funny at all.

They handed out leaflets, links to websites, contacts for charities that could help. You read everything several times because it was increasingly hard to take in information even then, particularly about unfamiliar things. James read them to you; you read them together. There were endless conversations with specialists, support workers, and with the lovely lady from the charity. You wanted, no, you needed to understand what was coming, to be prepared for whatever was ahead. Though deep down, you knew it was inevitable.

You sat down on a sunny afternoon when you realised that soon when this illness had really taken hold, you would forget that you had grandchildren, forget even your children. You've spent a long time trying and failing to come to terms with the unhappy truth that the ones you love the most would eventually become strangers to you. You sat down at the battered old writing desk (inherited from your mother) and wrote yourself a series of letters, reminders of your most precious memories, and James promised that when the time came, he would return them.

When you wrote these words to yourself, you hoped that they wouldn't upset you too much, that they wouldn't scare the woman you would become. Don't cry. As your mother used to say, "Crying takes away the energy you need to fight." Keep reading. No one knows you as well as you know yourself, and as long as you are still there, still in a world where you have your family behind you, there will be a part of you that knows that you can do this, you can still be strong, still hold on. Hold on. Hold on to James; he's got you.

James has been the love of your life; your soul

mate and your best friend. He has been your most loyal and committed companion, and you love him as much as he still loves you. You've spent many hours staring into those gentle green eyes of his, holding that labourer's hand that touches you so softly. You've raised your three beautiful children and welcomed seven gorgeous grandchildren into your family. Your family have been your strength, and you are more proud of them than words can say.

James was your first real love, and although it was a short courtship, it wasn't wholly love at first sight. You met each other at the wedding of your cousin Helen to an old school friend of his. You were sitting next to each other at the reception, and for the first hour, you barely exchanged words. That wasn't for want of trying on your behalf, but other than a polite "Nice to meet you.", James sat silent, too shy to join in with the animated conversation amongst the guests on your table. You quite liked the look of him, despite the way he fidgeted in his seat, obviously uncomfortable in his smart suit. You liked the way he wore his hair slightly longer than fashionable and how he seemed to be listening intently to the conversation around him, even as he remained mute. He's always been like that. Quiet, not shy, and observant, taking in the world around him, considering, gathering his thoughts and words, thinking about what he wants to say. He sometimes jokes that he's so quiet because you are always talking. He "never gets a word in edgeways" to use an old cliché! Your father used to say that you never had a thought cross your mind that didn't immediately fly out of your mouth, but he meant it affectionately, even if it did sting on occasion.

Back to James – you'd almost given up on engaging him in conversation when Helen wandered over to your table, as she circulated amongst her guests between courses. "Wonderful!" she'd exclaimed. "I knew you two would get along!" (she obviously hadn't noticed his silence). "Sarah," she continued, "you and James have so much in common!" You were a bit bemused – your table had been chattering about several interesting subjects, and he'd yet to comment on any of them.

"Really?" you'd replied. "Like what?" You were genuinely curious, keen to get this handsome stranger chatting.

"Oh, all sorts," she added. "James likes old stuff too – don't you, James?"

His polite smile quirked into a grin at that. "Old stuff?" he asked.

"Yes, those old-fashioned books and things," she explained before turning to speak to another guest. His eyes crinkled, and his smile grew – her words had sparked some interest. She'd given you an opening, and you took it. And she was right; you do have a lot in common. As well as a love of classical literature, you share a love of old movies and spent the afternoon discussing your favourites. By the time the waiters had cleared away the coffee cups and started moving the tables to make way for the dancing, you were already falling for him. He wasn't much of a dancer, though he's improved slightly over the years with your guidance. As he held you in his arms and awkwardly swirled you around the dance floor, you knew he was special.

At the end of the evening, you agreed to meet him the following week. He bought tickets at the Empire to see a screening of *The Wizard of Oz*, one of your favourites. You shared popcorn and lost yourselves in the story, and he surprised you when he confidently held your hand, and you wondered how you ever thought he was shy. As Dorothy returned home from her adventures, you snuck a look at James, only to find him looking right back. You realised that you wanted to share an adventure of your own with him. And what an adventure it has been! After the film, he walked you home (the long way round), and you talked about everything and nothing. When it was time to say good night, he kissed you chastely on the cheek and thanked you for a lovely night. You laughed at his reserve and pulled him into your first real kiss. It was wonderful. As the butterflies in your tummy fluttered, your heart raced. The kiss didn't last as long as you'd have liked, but when you opened your eyes, you met that look, which told you everything you needed to know without words. That look which told you that he felt the same way as you – that look

– that he gave you just a few moments ago when he held out this letter.

He will struggle once you start to forget him. It will break his heart, as it is breaking yours. Yours has been a happy marriage. You have always been there for each other. In good times and bad, just as he is here for you now. You've called him many things over the years: your rock, your foundation, your reason for getting up every morning, and yes, you've even called him a "stubborn old fool" at times. You've had your arguments, just like any other couple, and there are lots of things you've disagreed on. But the one thing you've always agreed on, that you promised each other on your wedding day, and on the day you were diagnosed, was "in sickness and in health". He's not going anywhere. When you wrote this, the idea that scared you most was that your symptoms would get so severe that you'd forget so much, it would all become too much for him. He's promised you, over and over, that no matter what, he will be there. You'll know, from the fact that he's with you now, having given you this to read, that he's keeping that promise.

It was Claire from the charity that gave you the idea to write this. Well, not this specifically. She was explaining the importance of planning ahead. She meant things like a will, organising a Power of Attorney, and other financial matters. She said it was best to write these things down. You've done all that and more. You've made your children promise that when they see that you and James aren't coping very well at home, they will make sure you both get the proper help you need. Together, you've picked out a nursing home. You were drawn to the one with the beautiful garden, full of flowers and bird tables. It might even be the garden that you can see outside the window of the room you are in now. James was insistent that he would care for you himself, in the home you've shared since before Matthew was born, but Claire helped persuade him that at some point, you might need more than even his huge heart can give.

Then, although you had taken care of all the formal things, you found that you weren't quite finished. You want to remind yourself of everything you can – all of what you and James have shared. You've written a few more of these letters, describing important events: your wedding day, the births of each of your children, your grandchildren. You may have already read some of them. There is so much more you don't want to forget, more than you could ever put down on paper. So, although he's never been a man of many words, you've agreed that James will tell you stories, like the ones you both love to read. The stories he tells you, the ones he already has, and the ones he'll tell you tomorrow and the next day and the day after that – they are YOUR stories. They are the stories of your lives together, of the adventures you've had, of the places you've been. They will be the tales of the people you have known; of those you have loved. They will be about your family, your friends, your dramas, and your ordinary days. There will be happy ones, and maybe some will be sad. Listen to them. Hold them in your heart and be strong.

Don't be scared, not of him, or of forgetting. He will remember everything for you both.

About the author

Michelle Adams lives on Anglesey, North Wales. Since turning 40 a few years ago, she has returned to study and is currently a student with The Open University, studying towards a BA in Arts & Humanities (English Language & Creative Writing).

Marmalade

June Webber

Bitter orange

Annie's dream was interrupted by the sound of explosives and a furry bundle jumping on her bed miaowing. Was it a gas main or a gun fight, she wondered? She dimly recalled her mother carrying her to the air raid shelter during the Blitz. Timidly she drew back the curtain and peered out. Streaks of fire illuminated the sky bursting into stars, signalling the start of 2020. Annie's annoyance turned to resolution. This year she would win the Nell Gwynn Cup for marmalade at the summer fête. She had been runner-up to Marjorie Fortescue-Smythe for the previous four years, and now it was her turn! She never understood why the judge preferred Marjorie's anaemic offering to her rich golden preserve. Annie would have suspected sexual favours, but no man would be tempted by Marjorie's austere looks, so it must be poor judgement. This year, however, Annie had a new secret recipe and there was a new judge. She drifted back to sleep, dreaming of holding aloft the shining silver cup to the applause of all the villagers. It would be engraved with **her** name and sit proudly on **her** sideboard, and her photograph would appear in the local paper.

As soon as they appeared in the shops, Annie

searched for the ripest, juiciest oranges capturing the hot sun of Seville. She had never been further south than Bournemouth, but had seen pictures in magazines of Seville Cathedral, Flamenco dancers and orange trees. She sought out plump lemons and preserving sugar and wheeled it all back home in her shopping trolley. After a refreshing cup of tea, she got out the preserving pan inherited from her mother, which Annie's brother called the witch's cauldron. She set to work squeezing the juice and slicing the peel into thin slivers. Soon the liquid was bubbling away thickening to a rich amber colour, the citrus aroma permeating the kitchen. She lined up the warm, sterilised jars and carefully filled each, sealing with rounds of cellophane and rubber bands. The jars were labelled and lined up on the larder shelf awaiting judgement.

Annie suspected that Marjorie added some secret ingredient to her marmalade to impress the judge, perhaps sherry. That came from Spain, didn't it? She watched for Marjorie to wheel out her recycling bin and draw the curtains. Cautiously Annie crossed the road, lifted the bin lid, and on top of the milk bottles, yoghurt pots and copies of The Times, was an empty can of Ma Made, not even rinsed out. Triumphantly she seized the evidence and scurried back home to telephone the chairman of the fête committee, Councillor Higginson, interrupting his favourite television programme.

"Good evening Councillor I wish to make a

complaint. I have evidence that Marjorie Fortescue-Smythe has cheated by using Ma Made instead of making her marmalade herself. I think she should be disqualified!"

The chairman checked the competition rules. "It doesn't say anything here about how the marmalade is prepared. It just says a jar of marmalade."

"Well, I've spent hours cutting up fresh oranges, and all she's had to do is open a tin." Annie slammed down the phone.

The day of the fête approached. Annie tasted one of the jars and the marmalade was delicious, her best yet. She decided to take a jar to her cousin at the far side of the village, who was very partial to marmalade and had not been out since the start of lockdown. On her way, she glanced at the village noticeboard and could scarcely believe her eyes.

> **Due to Corona virus, we have regrettably had to cancel this year's summer fête. Apologies to all our residents. Last year's winners may retain their cups for another year.**

Annie picked up her precious jar of marmalade and angrily hurled it at the noticeboard.

About the author
June Webber lives in Dorset and is a member of three online writing groups. She writes short stories, poetry, and flash fiction. She has had one story on *CaféLit* and contributed a chapter to *Bus Pass Britain Rides Again*.

A Scratch for an Itch

Helen Kreeger

Bitter lemon

"It itches likes mad!"

"Probably just wax."

"Something's in there."

"Yes, your finger."

"No, something else."

"Go to the nurse; she'll syringe your ears."

"Don't like the sound of that."

"I don't like the look of you digging in your ear! And don't use up all my cotton buds."

"Is that all the sympathy I get?"

"Are you serious?"

"Forget it."

"You arrive home last night smelling of some woman's nasty perfume and you want me to be sympathetic?"

"It's not what you think."

"It never is, darling, and yet we find ourselves here again."

"You women, you over-react about these things!"

"*These things*?"

"Just office life. Hell! You must have something for this blasted ear?"

"Don't swear."

"Blast, blast, blast!"

"Very juvenile. You know, I worked in an office for years, and didn't indulge in *these things*."

"I should hope not! Come over here."

"Why? So you can get round me? So I can forgive you, again?"

"I need you to look in my ear."

"What!… OK, let me see."

"There's something in there isn't there?"

"Stop digging and turn your head towards the window. Why do you do it?"

"Because it itches like hell."

"You know what I'm talking about. Aren't you a bit long-in-the-tooth to still be chasing girls?"

"It's not planned. I'm not looking for it. See anything?"

"Maybe… pass me those cotton buds. So why do it?"

"Those girls… they'll do anything for promotion. Ouch! What was that?"

"Sorry. Doesn't look like wax."

"I knew it! What is it?"

"Don't move! And keep your fingers out!"

"Hurry up!"

"I could just let you go to the nurse."

"For God's sake, woman, just get it out!"

"All right, hold still. So, tell me why you have to screw around."

"Now?"

"Why not? You usually escape to some appointment

or other when I bring it up. If you want your ear sorted you'd better start talking."

"I do love you, you know."

"I've heard all that before – doesn't give me answers."

"It's... a man thing. When you're offered free sweets you can't say no."

"That sounds more like a child thing. Ever tried to say no?"

"If you knew the number of women I've turned down..."

"It's the ones you don't turn down I'm interested in. I don't know what's in there, but it doesn't want to come out without a fight."

"Can you reach it?"

"Maybe you should go to the nurse."

"I don't have time to sit in a waiting room full of sickies waiting for Sharon to call my name."

"Sharon? That's her name is it?"

"What?"

"Nurse Robinson, at the clinic. Nobody calls her Sharon."

"Well, you know me, first name terms with everyone."

"Yes, I do know you. So, when were you last at the doctors' clinic?"

"Can't you just get out whatever's in there?"

"That's what I've been trying... Jesus! What is that?"

"What! What is it?'

"It's moving!"

"Oh, hell, get it out! I feel sick"

"I can't. Oh… it's too…"

"Please, do something!"

"It's… coming out. Oh, dear God, it's…"

"Help me, please. My chest… call the doctor, please."

"… enormous! Here you are – wax. Bloody big lump of it. You're looking a bit pale. Shall I call Sharon?"

About the author

Helen Kreeger was born and raised in London, but has lived elsewhere for many years. She has been published in *Blunt Moms* (USA), *ARC 25, 26 and 27* (Israel), *Writing District*, (UK), *Café Aphra* (USA), *Scrittura Lit Mag* (UK), *Free Flash Fiction*, and *With Painted Words* (UK).

SEPTEMBER

I chose A Piece of the Land I Came From *because the more I read it the more it captured me. The factual style of writing was engaging. Great title made me want to read on. The emphasis is on family and roots which are symbolised by the amber native to Poland. It spoke of displacement through conflict and denial and re-engagement with the past. The protagonist, through determination, succeeds in finding her place in the world. Keeping on the theme of family,* The Winter Thaw *was chosen because it is upbeat. In this inter-generational story, Raylene Clark, is widowed, lonely and worried about how to keep the snow, which her husband had always shovelled, at bay. This becomes the metaphor for life without him. Cary, a young boy, comes from a large family and longs for some peace away from his boisterous, noisy brothers and sisters. Carl is kind and funny, Raylene is kind and nurturing. Theirs becomes a symbiotic relationship and the solution to their individual problems. Both the stories are positive and look forward to a better future for the characters.*

About the editor

Liz Cox lives in the beautiful Yorkshire Dales where she writes short stories and poetry.

A Piece of the Land I Came From

Ann Christine Tabaka

Leroux Jezynowka Polish blackberry brandy

Most of her life, Anna grew up not knowing any family, except her immediate one. Her father was a stern and angry man, he was very private about his life. Teodor was born in a coal mining town in Pennsylvania, but grew up in war-torn Poland from 1910 to 1925. His mother Anna (her namesake) took him back to her family village to show him off, which was the tradition among the Polish settlers that came to America. Shortly after arriving in Poland, his brother Wawrzyniec was born in the small rural village outside of the town of Sokołów Podlaski, in 1911. When they were finally able to return to America in 1925, they did not know any English, and had very little schooling because of the war. They were put in second grade since they knew so little. All the other children made fun of them, because they were so much older. Teodor left school in 7th grade because he was so embarrassed. He never did continue his education, and did menial labor his entire life.

Anna had two older brothers. They were much older than she was, and left the house as soon as they were old enough to do so. Teodor was a harsh father and would be violent much of the time. The only other family Anna knew was her paternal grandmother, Anna, whom she always called Babci. Her paternal grandfather (Dziadek in Polish), Adam died when she was two years old. Her "Uncle Larry" died at his own hands before she was born. Her mother Marion was given away at birth, so she never knew anything about her maternal family, not even her adoptive one. Teodor did not want any contact with anyone from his heritage. He was an American now, and none of his children would even be allowed to learn the Polish language. This made things very hard since they were close to their Babci, and she spoke very little English. Of course, Marion and Teodor would speak Polish whenever they did not want the children to understand what they were saying.

Years passed, and everyone in the immediate family left, so they grew apart. Teodor died early from his disease, and Anna worked hard to improve her life and become a career woman. She thought very little about family or heritage, since she never knew anything about hers. Anna had her own family now. She was always a little envious of how close her husband's family was, and how much they knew about their history, but there was no use being too-upset about something she never had in the first place. She remained very close with her mother, and her middle brother, but her oldest brother and his family had distanced himself from everyone when their father was still alive, and they never became close again. That is, until Teodor, Jr. passed away in his late 40s, and one of his daughters contacted Anna to ask her a favor.

One of Anna's nieces, Carolyn, asked if I knew anything about her father, Teodor Jr.'s side of the family. Carolyn's son was doing a school genealogy project, and they found information on her mother's family back several hundred years, but had nothing for her father. Anna knew nothing about the family history, but said that she would see what she could do.

Anna's mother, Marion, had been suffering from stroke induced dementia for several years, and it was getting worse. Anna and her husband had to place Marion someplace where she would be safe and get the medical care she needed. They had to sell her old ruin of a house and move her to an assisted living situation. It was a long painful battle to go through all the clutter Marion had accumulated over the years. Dementia has a way of making its victim collect things: newspapers, charity mail requests, old grocery receipts, etc. It took Anna many hours of many weeks, into many months, to go through as much of her mother's precious collections as she had the energy to manage. She now knows that she threw out many things that she regrets today. It came down to survival once again, as she hauled out huge trash bags full of papers that she didn't even give a second glance to. She was in emotional pain because of my mother's situation, and physically exhausted from the labor of clearing out the house. But still somehow, she managed to mindlessly throw a number of items into several boxes to take to her house. She didn't even remember what she took or why she took them. She still thinks her Babcia was watching over her shoulder, whispering in her ear to "save that photograph and keep those pieces of paper."

Anna was later surprised when looking through the boxes to find out that she had actually saved some important items that she was eternally grateful for. Because of those few precious documents and pictures, she was able to start searching for who her ancestors were. She was going to help Teodor Jr.'s kids find their father's family after all.

Over the next three years Anna wrote to every Hall of Records, and church she could contact from the information that she had on birth, marriage, and death certificates that she had found at her mother's house. It was an arduous task researching addresses, typing letters, and paying all the fees. Fifteen dollars, here, twenty dollars there, twenty-five dollars, and so on, and many times with no results at all. But, in those times when she did have a certified document sent back to her, she felt as if she hit a gold mine. Anna was elated – she had FAMILY! Family all over the USA, in Poland, and many other countries as well.

Writing to Poland was the hardest part. She had the names of villages and relatives from some of the documents that she obtained in America, but so many of the Polish villages had changed names during the many wars it underwent. Not to mention Anna could not read or write Polish. Thank goodness that Anna lived in the late twentieth century, and thank goodness for computers. She found Polish Genealogy websites on the Internet. They were extremely helpful, and even had form letters she could print out and start sending to Poland. Little did Ann know that that was just the beginning of her troubles. Now, she had to find someone to translate the replies, and to convert US dollars into Polish money. Because of the Polish Genealogy sites, Anna found Christina, who lived in Warsaw. Christina was born in the USA, but her parents were from Slavic countries, so Christina decided to get her degrees in languages, Polish, and five other foreign languages. Christina moved to Warsaw and did translations for the University there. Christina was a language whiz, and very knowledgeable about Polish customs and history.

The Polish genealogy mailing list discussed many different subjects that pertain to all things Polish. Someone on the list was asking about the origin of a piece of amber jewelry that an ancestor had. They wanted to know what part of Poland most amber came from. Until that particular post, Anna was not aware that most amber was from Poland and the area around the Baltic Sea. She was never interested in amber before. She was more interested in rubies and precious gemstones. Anna's Babcia always treasured her strand of amber beads, but Anna never thought much of that "brown" necklace. All of a sudden, Anna was curious to know more about amber. She began to think it would be nice to have a piece of jewelry that came from the land of her ancestors, a "piece of the land she came from."

Amber is the fossilized resin of ancient trees, which formed through a natural polymerization of the original organic compounds. Most of the world's amber is in the range of 30-90 million years old. Jewelry made from amber comes in several colors, including butterscotch, cognac, cherry, and green. It can be transparent or opaque, polished or rough, faceted or free form. Many amber pieces have been carved and inlaid to make cameos. Sometimes, it even has a fossilized ancient insect or piece of vegetation encased inside it. Best of all, amber jewelry is relatively inexpensive.

Now Anna wanted some amber jewelry for herself. She also thought it would be nice to purchase some amber earrings as a thank you gift for her Polish coworker who had been translating all those letters for her before she found Christina. She decided to ask her new found friend in Poland if she could recommend a place to buy some authentic Polish amber jewelry.

Christina seemed delighted. In fact, she informed Anna that the very day she asked her, she had just gone out and purchased her very first piece of amber jewelry for herself. It was a green amber stone in silver pendant. She thought it was extraordinary that Anna had asked her on that exact day. She mentioned that she does not usually buy jewelry for herself, so it was a special treat.

Christina lives in Warsaw's Old Town. She told Anna there are many shops there that sell amber. She offered to pick something out for Anna in one of the shops and send it to her. She mentioned that the amber and silver jewelry in Poland was less expensive than what could be found in the USA. Anna could pay her for it afterwards. Anna wasn't sure if she wanted a more traditional necklace of beads, the type that her Babci wore, or something more modern. She started to look around the Internet, and found so many styles of necklaces and pendants, that she decided she might eventually have to have several. Anna sent pictures of a few styles that she liked to Christina, and told her to choose something she would like herself. She figured that anyone named Christina from Slavic background had to have good taste. After all, Anna's middle name was Christine also.

Christina decided that the green amber pendant that she had bought for herself must have been meant for Anna. She said it was fate, since Anna had asked her about amber on the very same day that she purchased it. So now Anna had a "piece of the land she came from" actually purchased in Poland. What made it even more special is that Christina had worn it once already. So, when Anna wore the amber, she felt as if she was actually touching her dear friend Christina.

And so began another chapter for Anna. So much had happened in the past three years. Finally, at the age of fifty, Anna had family, and she held a tiny piece of Poland in her hand. As she lovingly touched to precious pendant on her silver chain, Anna wondered what new and exciting things awaited her around the next corner.

About the author

Ann Christine Tabaka was nominated for the 2017 Pushcart Prize in Poetry. Winner of Spillwords Press 2020 Publication of the Year. Her bio is featured in the *Who's Who of Emerging Writers 2020 and 2021*, published by *Sweetycat Press*. She is the author of 14 poetry books.

The Winter Thaw

Dawn DeBraal

Hot cocoa

Raylene stood looking out her window as the snow came down lazily. Normally she loved to see this kind of weather, likening it to snow globe magic, but not now. Tom was gone he was the one who went out and shoveled it, plowed it, conquered it with his snowblower. She only had use of the mighty snow shovel.

They predicted thirteen inches of the white stuff. Raylene had been going out and shoveling the driveway every few hours so she could keep up with it.

It was only January, and already she was sick of winter. There were months to go yet. She drank the rest of her coffee, grabbed her boots, pulled them on, and went outside to start the process of removing the snow again from her front steps and then down the driveway.

"Hi, Mrs Clark," her neighbor Cary Gorman stood before her with a snow shovel in hand.

"Hello, Cary!"

"I've come to help you with the driveway. You don't have to pay me. I'm just being neighborly, is all." His statement made her chuckle.

"Well, that sounds wonderful. How about you

help me, and we have some hot cocoa?" Cary smiled, running down the driveway with the snow shovel. Youth is wasted on the young, she thought. Cary worked like he was possessed. Raylene marveled at what a young child could do. Before she knew it, another few inches of the white stuff, was cleared from the drive.

"Come in for that cocoa." Raylene held the door open. Cary ducked inside where it was warm. Kermit, the old golden retriever, came up with his tail wagging and greeted Cary.

"Hello Kermit, good boy." Cary took off his coat and boots and climbed up to Raylene's island, waiting patiently while she warmed the cocoa.

"It must get pretty lonely here without Mr Clark." What a sweet boy.

"I am glad that I have Kermit. You are right. It has been lonely without my Tom. But it is what it is."

"What does that mean?" Cary looked at her inquisitively.

"That means there is nothing we can do about a situation, so you need to make the most of it."

"Like shoveling together and making hot cocoa?"

"Exactly." Cary made Raylene smile again. She was glad for his company.

"How come you don't have kids, Mrs Clark?"

"God never saw fit to bless us with any."

Cary thought about that for a moment. "Well, God has blessed my mom and dad way too much."

This made Raylene laugh out loud, for the Gorman family had four boys and two girls. Cary, being the youngest.

"Not too much, just the right amount." Raylene put the cocoa down in front of him.

"Do you have any graham crackers?"

Raylene went to the cupboard and pulled the waxed paper-wrapped crackers out and opened them. They each took one, dipping it into the hot chocolate. Cary sighed with contentment.

"This was worth all the work! You know, my grandma died last year. I don't have one anymore."

"I know. I was sorry to hear that. I knew Sophie; she was a friend of mine."

"You knew my grandmother?" Cary's eyes got big.

"Yes, I did, and your grandfather, too."

"What were they like in the olden days?" Cary dunked his cracker into the hot chocolate, taking another bite.

"Your grandparents were quite the dancers. They took lessons from a school. They entered competitions all over the state. Your grandmother had the most beautiful dresses that she wore with flouncy skirts. They were quite good, as I recall."

"Dancing is for sissies."

"Oh no, you have to be in top shape. It takes a lot of strength and stamina. They won trophies. They had a case in the living room full of them."

"I remember that! I thought they were bowling trophies like my dad's."

"Oh no, your grandparents were State Champions; they were so good."

"I like that story! It's so quiet here. At my house, it's noisy, noisy, noisy, all the time. I can't think."

"Well, you can come over anytime you need quiet. My house is just too quiet sometimes. Kermit doesn't make much noise."

"Yes, he's a quiet dog. Do you like having noise in your house?"

"Sometimes. Why do you ask?"

"My mom tells me I'm pretty noisy. I try not to be, but you have to be heard above the others."

That made Raylene laugh again. "Yes, I suppose you do." The phone rang. "Hello, Cora. Yes, he's here. He helped me shovel my drive. No, he's no bother. I enjoy the company. Yes, I will tell him."

"That was your mom, she said when you are done here, you should come straight home."

"I'm surprised she noticed I was gone."

"Oh, mothers notice. Why do you think a mother duck will notice when one of her ducklings are missing, and she'll have a dozen of them?"

"I never thought about it. Ducks can count?"

"I don't know if they can or not, but they know each one of their children, so they instinctively know when one is missing."

"Mrs Clark, you sure know a lot of things."

"I do, that I do." He'd made her smile again. He was such a wonderful boy. Raylene opened her purse and took out five dollars, handing it over to Cary.

"I don't want any money, Mrs Clark, but if it's okay with you, I'd like to come and listen to your quiet sometimes and drink hot chocolate?"

"I'd like that very much, Cary. I tell you what. I will put your earnings on an account."

"What does that mean?"

"Is there something you want, a toy or something?"

"Yes, it's a video game, but it costs forty dollars."

"Alright, we will keep tabs. Every time you shovel my driveway or do a chore, I will add some money into your account with me." She pulled out a sheet of paper and wrote the date in one column, and shoveled snow, and in the other she wrote five dollars. She taped it on the inside cupboard door. "When you've earned forty dollars, and your mom and dad say it's okay, we'll get that game."

Cary's smile was as big as his heart. "That's a great idea. Can I come back tomorrow?"

"Yes, you may come anytime your parents say it's okay."

"Mrs Clark, since you have no kids, and I don't have a grandma anymore, would you like to be my grandma? I could call you Grandma Clark."

Raylene's heart broke open. She had been so closed off since Tom died. "I would like that very much."

"Can I give you a hug?"

"I'd like that very much." Raylene closed her eyes and let his affection sink in. He probably would lose interest in her in a short time, but for now, she was going to enjoy his company.

"Well, I better get home." He pulled on his boots and coat. "Bye, Grandma Clark, see you tomorrow." Raylene watched him run down the driveway with the shovel in his hand. Her heart was full. In the winter of her life, she'd found a bit of spring.

About the author

Dawn DeBraal lives in rural Wisconsin with her husband, Red, two rescue dogs, and a stray cat. She has published over 500 stories, poems, and drabbles in several online magazines and anthologies.

OCTOBER

A Pet Shop Parable *surprised me. I'm not always a fan of "clever twists", as they can feel like gimmicks if poorly handled, but I enjoyed this. It moves from what seems to be a cute animal story to canine horror by the end… and may have almost made me spurt my coffee everywhere!*

Pebbles on the Beach *shows the personal loss of a home, triggering an epiphany – the sobering acknowledgement of how much damage humankind has done, and is doing, to our world. I chose the story because it made me think and kept coming back to me, long after I finished reading it.*

I put Pick Telephones on the Moon *on my "yes" list instantly. It was touching and understated, a sweet romance. Wallace painted this story with a light hand, using lively descriptions of colour, giving us just enough and not too much. Beautiful.*

For its uniqueness, Furniture *was another instant "yes". A piece of absurd flash fiction, featuring talking furniture and dark espresso prose… What's not to love?*

About the editor
Hannah Retallick, writer and editor from North Wales.

www.hannahretallick.co.uk/

A Pet Shop Parable

Ken Goldman

Margarita: fun, but with a sneaky tang

How much is that doggie in the window?
– Hit Song by Patti Page (1953)

A Madison Avenue executive might have called it a Kodak Moment. Maybe a song lyricist would have chronicled the instant with "These Are The Times of Your Life." The boy-and-his-dog event was pure Americana, and his interaction with the coal black terrier could have inspired a Rockwell painting.

The kid was maybe fourteen, and he had come with his father to Jonathan Somers' animal shelter to find a pet among the dozens on display within the large inner shop. Passing cages of cockers and pugs, young shepherds and mixed breeds, he finally stopped before the screen mesh enclosure containing four tiny wire-haired pups. One dog jumped and rolled at the sight of the young man's interest, yelping excitedly at him through the screen. Jonathan had spent a large part of his retirement income to experience moments like this, and he found himself smiling like a department store Santa whenever they occurred.

"Made a new friend, have you?" he asked the tousle-haired kid, already knowing the answer. He winked at the youth's father who stood in the far corner pretending to be absorbed in a young floppy-eared mutt. "Would you like to hold him?"

The kid's eyes told the old man all he needed to know. Jonathan unlocked the cage and scooped up the eager puppy in one motion, holding it out for him.

"This little fella isn't purebred, but he'll show you some fine times, I can guarantee—"

The kid looked at Somers quizzically.

"No. Not that one." He pointed back to the small cage where two other pups frolicked. A third sat shivering and alone by the far wall, a drab brown and spotted white creature of dubious lineage, unique from the others only because of its isolation from them.

"That one."

The old man thought the kid might be making a cruel joke, pulling his leg like smart-assed types sometimes did just to tease some poor animal. But the youth's expression did not suggest anything remotely frivolous in his decision.

From the day the mongrel had been weaned the splotched wire-hair never demonstrated the frisky behavior that most of the other kennel puppies did. Although not stricken with anything life-threatening, the mutt had been the runt of his litter and seemed to have trouble standing on all fours. There were state laws about selling such animals to the public, and a canine's defects had to be disclosed before making a sale. Of course, Jonathan would never stoop to deceptive behavior regardless of the humanitarian considerations some well-meaning types might have for purchasing imperfect animals as pets. Although he believed every dog deserved his fair shake at adoption, he knew the spotted pup was an unsuitable pet for an energetic young man. The boy had a right to know that.

Somers hoped the kid's father might intervene, but the man remained where he stood at the other end of the store. Jonathan would have to handle this delicate matter on his own.

"Look at his right rear leg, son. Can you see? That dog is lame. He won't be able to run. Not ever. He might make a fine pet for an elderly person, one who isn't able to play rough-and-tumble with a dog the way an active young man like yourself can. That's why I keep him out here on display. Terriers are popular with just about everyone, and he's got maybe half a terrier in his blood. He'll find a home, all right, one where he'll be happy. But I wouldn't suggest to a boy your age--"

"Can I hold him?"

Somers' first impulse was to refuse the kid's request outright. He had run the shelter long enough to know when a match just didn't feel comfortable regardless of the initial appeal. It wasn't much different from falling in love at first sight. The lisp you once thought was so endearing later makes you want to go for your woman's throat every time she accidentally spits into your eye. But he could see the young man had already made up his mind.

"No law against holding him, I suppose." Somers slipped his hand past the screen mesh.

The pup looked dully at Jonathan's open palm but made no effort to resist. Somers could not tell whether the animal were completely docile or simply too weak to do anything else but shake. The maybe-terrier struggled to its feet just before the old man lifted it from the cage.

The boy took the pup into his arms as if he held a precious gift. The dog's shivering slackened while he stroked its muzzle and the puny tail even managed a respectable wag.

"He's perfect."

Jonathan hated the words he had to say.

"No, son. He's not."

The boy's father appeared alongside Somers so abruptly it seemed he had sneaked up behind him. Placing an arm around the youth he joined his son in stroking the puppy's wiry fur. An amazing thing happened, a disquieting miracle that Somers had not expected. The dog licked at the boy's face with an enthusiasm the old man had never seen the animal demonstrate.

The father saw it too and turned toward Somers. "My Nat's looked at so many dogs today. This is the first one he's shown any real interest in."

Although that interest clearly went two ways,

Somers believed a little diplomacy was in order. Clearly the father was not going to dissuade young Nathaniel from his selection. Jonathan had the dog's welfare to consider also. By next week the boy could have second thoughts. A rejected animal might whine for days, often would refuse food or mistrust displays of affection toward it. People's pity for helpless creatures created emotional blind spots, and families with the best intentions were the ones most guilty of not considering an animal's best interests.

"Why not look at some other pups before making your decision?" Somers suggested.

Nathaniel did not hear a single word.

The father caught Jonathan's eye. An almost imperceptible shake of his head implied that Somers should look towards the boy's right shoe. The old man's mouth opened as if he might speak, but he said nothing. Somehow he hadn't noticed it before.

A leg brace peeked through the boy's denims.

"I wouldn't worry about the dog's being physically challenged, Mr Somers. Just look at the two of them. It's like the rest of the world has gone and disappeared. The important thing is that an animal teaches a boy love and responsibility, don't you think? Nathaniel is paying for his pet out of his own pocket, and I believe that's a pretty good start. You can see how that pup makes my boy feel. Can anyone ask more of an animal?"

Jonathan smiled weakly, hoping his embarrassment didn't show. He was happy to concede this one.

"How much do you want for this pup, Mr Somers?" the boy asked.

Jonathan Somers didn't believe in price fixing when it came to making a good match. He smiled at the father and leaned toward the boy as if sharing a confidence. "I manage this shelter through donations, Nathaniel. Whatever you feel is appropriate will do just fine."

The boy rifled through his pockets and held out a crumpled ten dollar bill with some coins.

"It's all I have."

"More than enough," Somers said. "You've selected a fine dog today, son."

Smiles all around.

And again the kid's eyes said it all.

Every boy should have a pet.

These were the father's thoughts while he watched his son fetch the large plastic dish from the pantry in preparation for his new companion's first meal in their home. From the start this project was his and his alone. Nathaniel would have it no other way.

"I'm calling him Rusty, Dad. What do you think?"

"Rusty it is, then. You did a good thing today, son. I just wanted you to know."

The boy beamed with pride as he slid off the leg brace.

"I hated wearing this thing just to get a fair price from the old guy."

"Elderly people are usually generous with their pity, and we have to cut some corners if we're going to keep Rusty. I won't have you stealing strays off the street, Nat. Some things just aren't right. But there's not a thing wrong with being a shrewd shopper. Besides, your little wiry pal here would've been taking the big sleep soon enough. Who's going to buy a mutt that can't walk a straight line? There's that to consider too."

The boy nodded his agreement.

"You'll come with me tomorrow?"

"Keep that leg brace well oiled, son. There's kennels and pet shops just about everywhere. We'll pay each a visit or two, maybe even take the trailer and see some of the country while we're at it. But right now I'll bet Rusty is one hungry animal."

Nathaniel again nodded agreement. He picked up the large dish and placed the lame little mutt inside.

"I want to feed him myself, Dad. Okay?"

"Fine with me. I'd like to watch, if it's all right."

His son nodded as he carried the pup down the stairs to the large glass enclosed cage he had constructed in the basement for his new companion.

His father had been correct.

Nathaniel's pet boa constrictor Rusty was hungry as hell.

About the author

Ken Goldman, a former Philadelphia English and Film Studies teacher, is an Active member of the Horror Writers Association. He has written six books: *You Had Me at Arrgh!!*, *Donny Doesn't Live Here Anymore*, *Star-crossed*, *Desiree*, *Of a Feather*, and *Sinkhole*.

Pebbles on the Beach

Kevin Wood

Jasmine tea

I'd heard the news. And it was pretty bad. But I'd decided to go down the Cliff Road to see for myself. It took less than ten minutes before I arrived in the area and looking across the bay towards Dante's Cliff. I could see it was all true.

Overnight the cliff edge had broken away and taken with it about twenty to thirty yards of land. This devastation had meant that my childhood home had gone and was now nothing more than debris strewn across the beach at the foot of the Cliff. It was shocking and brought a lump to my throat. It felt like all my childhood memories had been swept away in one horrendous rockfall.

As I looked on my mind drifted back to those memories playing in our beautiful cliff top garden. In those days the edge seemed so far away. And beyond it we could look across the bay and out to sea. It was idyllic.

The garden, of course, is now gone. Much of it over recent years and then the remainder vanished shortly after we finally moved away last year. The Council had constantly warned us about the eroding rock getting closer to our home and sure enough once we had moved more of it fell taking the rest of the garden with it.

Now this.

I watched on as all of that emotion and memories were coming flooding back to me. I was holding back the tears.

I closed my eyes.

When my eyes were opened, I saw a rainforest burning, laying waste to the trees, sending the wildlife scattering for safety. Fleeing for their lives where possible and for the others…? They would not be so fortunate. For them their homes were no more than ashes. I saw a young orangutan as its forest home was being destroyed and its habitat turned to dust. Then I saw a polar bear hunting on a melting icecap. Searching for food that could no longer be relied on in this changing environment. I saw an oil spill in the sea killing the fish, the seabirds and much of the beautiful creatures that found themselves caught in its wake. Floundering. Helpless.

And then, when I opened my eyes once more, I could feel their pain. The collective loss. Despair. I thought is this really what we have done to the world?

It appears that just as we have spent countless years attacking nature now nature was attacking us. Whether it is my old clifftop home or perhaps the lands that are being flooded by the melting icecaps that had cost the polar bear so dearly.

For humankind or for nature itself I felt the outcome seemed so bleak. Whether I mourn for the wildlife or the loss of my own home the result is the same for all of us. We are homeless.

I looked out across the bay and considered what we were leaving behind. Ashes are scattered across a broken forest. Dust is blowing in the breeze of a world in flames as we ignore the other animal and plant life with which we share this planet.

As the climate screams and temperatures soar.

Until now as below me I see my home reduced to mere pebbles on the beach.

About the author

Kevin Wood is a retired accountant from Basildon Essex. He has written an, as yet unpublished, octology of short stories titled *The Search for Ellie Babble*. He continues to write mainly short stories and poems.

Pink Telephones on the Moon

Jamie Wallace

Mocha latte: sweet, creamy goodness, with a little sting of espresso

He would miss the colors of Earth the most: the emerald waters of the river cutting through sandy banks, his wife's favorite coral pink lipstick, the orange autumn leaves against a stormy sky. The moon would be toneless in comparison. On the patio, Steve sat with his back to the green Florida foliage but kept a sharp mental picture filed away for future use.

Steve cleared his throat. Waiting for the countdown of his launch was like suffering the last moment of a perfect first date: the moment of deciding whether to lean in for a kiss or quietly walk away. His watch ticked off the seconds.

Sitting across from Steve was his wife, Clara. "Time's almost up. What do you have left to do before you go?" she asked.

Everything was packed, all words had been said, there was nothing left to do but wait for the jingle of the telephone. Steve's skin crawled with bottled up energy like ants on a forgotten piece of food.

"I just want to take in the colors," said Steve. The hotel room was on the other side of the open patio door. The color scheme of burnt orange and avocado green spun like a kaleidoscope.

A light pink telephone sat on the bedside table, mocking him with its silence. Ring, dammit, ring, he thought. His fingers drummed a staccato rhythm on his pant leg.

Clara smiled and shifted in her seat. When her polyester pant suit slid across the vinyl of the chair, it was like a bow skimming across a violin string. A soft breeze blew a puff of her scent, and he stole a lungful: Chanel No. 5 and Aqua Net. The ticking of Clara's fingers on the side of her glass vibrated through his brain, and as she hummed *Hey Jude*, he hummed along. The blue of her eyes swept him away like the ocean tide. With the blush of her cheek, bedroom memories rolled through his mind like a movie reel. An escaped piece of sunshine yellow hair swayed in the breeze. Time didn't matter anymore.

Steve grasped Clara's hands. A bit of dirt had wedged itself under her pinky nail. A half-smile played across his lips. "Didn't like the gardening gloves I picked out?" he asked.

"I love the feel of Earth in my hands."

The telephone rang with a shrill echo in the silent room.

Clara trembled. Letting go of her, Steve rose and walked into the room. Clara followed.

The telephone rang, again.

I don't have to answer it, thought Steve. Wavering thoughts rushed through his mind. Walk away with Clara. Be together. Start a family. Stay.

Another ring.

Rocket to the Moon. Make history. Give back to the human race. Leave.

"Steve."

The hum in Steve's mind calmed at the sound of Clara's firm tone.

Clara's lips were pressed in a hard line. Her eyes, bright with tears, were large. Without hesitation, she walked to the bedside table.

The telephone stopped mid ring.

"Hello? Yes, sir, understood." Hanging up the telephone, Clara turned to Steve. "It's time."

About the author

Jamie Wallace is new to writing. She is an avid reader, pursuing a bachelor's degree in Creative Writing. She lives in the United States with her husband, has an adoring Great Dane, and five children who are the reason she has to dye her hair.

Furniture

Clive Gresswell

Espresso, as it is short, sharp and very, very dark

Billy Small turned his key in the lock and entered his flat. He was exhausted as it was a hard slog at work that day. He sighed sidled into the kitchen and boiled water in the kettle for a Cuppa Soup. All set up for an evening of being a couch potato and watching a load of mindless television quiz shows he took his meagre tea into the front room and collapsed wheezing onto the settee. *What a bore*, he thought. He closed his eyes and heard a booming voice echo, "Hey, watch it fatso, you're quite heavy you know." Billy rubbed his eyes as if he'd been dreaming and leapt to his feet. Startled he looked around him but there was no other person to be seen. He hadn't recognized the voice either and wondered for a moment where it had come from. Then he hit his head with his hand and whispered to himself, "Of course, I remember now."

But he was definitely under the impression that he, his landlord and the furniture had all come to an agreement that they wouldn't trouble him anymore, and that was only a few days ago.

He remembered that first of all it was the settee which had piped up. He recalled distinctly that it happened on Tuesday of last week at about 6pm.

" 'Ere mate, take a weight off," the settee had said

and soon enough all the chairs and a table in the room were joining in hurling insults at him. If it wasn't criticisms of his size it was rudeness about his fashion sense or his balding hair. This was all too much. Worse than when mother was alive!

He tried hitting back saying the frayed furniture was nothing to write home about either, so there. But the furniture just laughed at him and told him he was going mad.

"Well, you lot are driving me to it," he countered.

Billy had tried reason last time and look where that had got him. There was nothing to do but eliminate the enemy. He went into the kitchen and taking the longest breadknife he could find marched back into the living room and swearing lunged at all the furniture, piercing the settee so the stuffing came out of it. The laughter of the furniture turned into loud screams. Afterwards Billy collapsed even more exhausted onto the floor. He heard a knock at the front door and then an urgent ringing of the doorbell. When he opened it his psychiatrist stood there flanked by two police officers. "So, it's furnitureside now is it Billy," said Dr Maudsley in his broad Scottish accent. "I think you'd better come with us."

Billy turned to get his coat but could still hear the furniture muttering in the background.

"He hasn't been right for years," said the table, and the others shouted out their agreement.

About the author

Clive enjoys writing metafictions and absurdist stories. He has a poetry MA and a BA (First Class) in Creative Writing from the University of Bedfordshire. His poems and short stories have appeared in many magazines and books from *BlazeVox* to *Tears in the Fence*. His latest book *Shadow Reel* is a 16,000-word prose poem published in March by *New Note Poetry* (online).

NOVEMBER

I wanted to choose stories that moved me and also others that made me smile or laugh. I like a balance in what I write and read.

The Stranger at the Feast *is a heart-warming tale of a woman getting her life back. Loved the ending of this. Served her ex right. Also good to see her finding her strength and making a new life for herself.*

Mrs Brown's Sideboard *is a wonderful portrait of life. I too remember sideboards like that. I thought Mrs Brown especially was sympathetically portrayed and I totally understand why she wanted that piece of furniture and wouldn't dream of getting rid of it.*

Dear. Ms. Ginger Snaps *is wonderful, quirky, funny and ticks all of my boxes. Great idea, well executed. (Oh and I love fruitcake – and ginger snaps).*

Outwitted, Outplayed, Outdone Your Honour *is fantastic. So funny. I can picture the court scenes and almost hear the voices of the characters. That's great writing.*

About the editor

Allison Symes, who loves quirky fiction, is published by *Chapeltown Books, CaféLit*, and *Bridge House Publishing*. Her flash fiction collections, *From Light to Dark and Back Again* and *Tripping the Flash Fantastic,* are available in Kindle and paperback. She writes weekly for online magazine, *Chandler's Ford Today,* on topics of interest to writers.

Allison also gives workshops on flash fiction on *Zoom* and in person where possible. She is a member of the *Society of Authors* and the *Association of Christian Writers*.

The Stranger at The Feast

Ann Bright

Gin and tonic

Linda stood looking at her reflection in the gilded full length mirror smoothing her hands over the white lace dress made especially for her and she didn't see the wide hips, the heavy breasts, the thickening waist, she saw a curvaceous, sexy, elegant, beautiful woman.

She slipped her feet into the satin court shoes-she was pretty sure they wouldn't last all day!-and picked up her bouquet of dried lavender. With a deep breath she left the dressing room and walked into the bedroom with its huge four poster bed, where her daughter, granddaughter, sisters and mum were waiting. They were a tight and powerful group these women, they had always been pillars of strength for each other, during the most difficult of times they listened together, they cried together and Linda's life would have taken a very different path if she hadn't always had them there to rely on. She had brought Sarah up as a single mum sheltered by the protective wall of her family. Although they had lived with her family until Sarah was old enough to go to school and Linda could work full time, although they had been secure and Sarah had received enough love for ten children, Linda had carried the weight of the shame of being an unmarried mother around her neck, dragging her head down, never feeling good enough to look people in the eye. She had had boyfriends in the past, but so many would be one date wonders when she revealed that she had a child. Occasionally a good one would come along who would talk of the future and making a family of the three of them, but her insecurities and scars of betrayal from the past saw her shut down and push them away.

Until Bill came along. Of course it didn't matter to him all these years later that she'd had a child out of wedlock; the world was a different place now and Bill wanted to be with Linda just as much as she wanted to be with him. This was no one-sided love affair destined to end in heartbreak. And he was pretty close to her idea of perfect-dependable, handsome, strong, so very kind, thoughtful, generous, loving, and he made her feel safe, thank cupid for e-harmony. Her life had always been a struggle and she'd been so lonely for so long, but then asking her came and for the first time since that first time, she'd let herself go. He was the right man for her and they'd met just at the right time in their lives.

The bridal party went to their seats leaving just Linda and her mum. The door opened as adagio for strings played. Linda and Bill's eyes met, his enormous smile matched her own and she saw him wipe away tears, this was the happiest moment of her life. And suddenly she couldn't wait to get to him, couldn't wait another minute to be his wife. It felt desperately important to her that she should belong to another, that they would belong to each other. She clasped her mum's hand and began the walk down the aisle towards her love, thankfully her mum's slow pace forced Linda to take her time so she could take it all in as she walked towards her future. Her people were on the left and she searched the smiling faces for Tracey, her oldest and best friend-there she was blowing her a kiss. They had always been single together, but Tracey had never had any trouble finding a mate, she was just a bit too wild to be tamed! The attractive man next to her looked familiar and Linda figured it must be her new Mr Right now, she said she'd be bringing him-she must have seen photos of them together on Facebook. Turning to the right there was all of her new family and Bill's friends that were now their friends.

Before she knew it the ceremony was over and she was walking back down the aisle on the arm of her new husband. She was a newlywed at 59! But she felt giddy as a bride of any age. They walked together between the applauding guests and made their way into the reception area. After the initial hugs it was time for photos, some inside, some outside in the hotel gardens. Glasses of champagne were passed round and the guests drifted off to the bar and the various comfy seating areas. Suddenly arms were around her; it was Tracey.

"You did it!! About time one of us did really," she laughed!

"We need a photo of just the two of us," Linda said and they looked for a pretty backdrop in the garden.

"Hey, could be you next – your new fella is pretty good looking, a bit of a change from some of your usual guys!"

"I didn't bring him. That's over. He was too boring, I think I'll go back to dating 35 year olds"

"So who was that next to you then? I thought I recognised him." Linda said.

"I dunno, but I'll tell you what, a couple of glasses of fizz I'll be hunting him down later," Tracey winked.

"So who is he then?" Linda wondered.

And then suddenly her past came screaming into her present. See needed some space, she needed to breathe. "I'm just going to the loo. We'll do our photo when I get back" and she set off towards the hotel but took a detour that led to a section of walled garden, the perfect place to hide and gather her thoughts.

She was 18 again and the most beautiful boy she'd ever seen was smiling at her across the club. She looked around, thinking Tracey must be standing behind her, but no, it was her he was looking at and now oh my god, he was walking over to her. He asked her to dance and pretty much from that moment on they were inseparable. He took her out for meals, with menus she'd couldn't understand of exquisite food so alien to what she was used to, they went to the theatre, out for drinks with his fancy friends in his little red convertible. If ever she felt out of place he just held her close and told her she was the most special, that she was better than anyone else, he was her passport to a different new world and she loved it. He took her shopping, spoiled her with the latest fashions. He was known in the best shops. They were in love and she was delirious, so when he suggested they have a weekend away, she knew what it meant, but was more than happy to go along with it because this was forever. And when she found out she was pregnant at 19, he was thrilled; they would get married, he said, money wasn't a problem, he worked for his father's company and had a very healthy trust fund that provided his comfortable lifestyle. She would have a custom-made dress, he said, that would hide any small bump that might be showing. They'd go on a luxurious honeymoon to Italy, he said, and then when they got back they'd move into a new flat together and prepare to become a family. It was a fairy tale come true and they wanted both sets of parents to find out on the same day, so she waited to tell her mum and dad until she'd had a chance to meet his parents. He assured her that although they'd be shocked they'd love her just as much as he did and everything would be fine. And it wouldn't make a difference if they weren't happy, because this was their lives and their future.

So Linda sat on the armchair in the bay window of the house she shared with three other girls from the office, waiting to be picked up to go and meet his parents. She was wearing a pale yellow full skirted, drop shoulder dress, with white lace trim and white shoes. She was holding a small white handbag and a pair of white lace gloves. She gripped them tightly; she was nervous but excited too. And she waited, and she waited. An hour had gone by and still no sign. She was getting worried. What if he'd had an accident? As the hours passed and the sun went down, the horror of reality started to dawn on her. He wasn't coming. As the hours became days she realised with a sickening feeling that she was alone.

"Linda"

There he was, this man who broke her and built her at the same time.

"I had to see you"

"Why? After all these years, why?"

"Because I had to say I'm sorry. It broke my heart to leave you but my parents threatened to cut me off if I didn't walk away from you. They sent me away."

"But we were in love. We were going to have a baby together. How did you just turn off your feelings, how could you stop caring?"

"But that's the point; I never stopped caring and

loving you and not a day goes by that I don't think about my child and how wonderful our lives would have been. I had to see if we still had a chance."

Linda bowed her head and tears fell silently. He took her in his arms and time melted away, she felt a surge of emotion as she held him, as though nothing had changed. She looked up into his deep blue eyes, but this time she wasn't mesmerised as she'd been all those years ago; this time she felt rage. He moved forward to kiss her and she placed her hands on his chest, roughly pushing him away.

"No, you don't get to come to me on my wedding day, when I've finally found the right man and try and turn my life upside down again. Walk away now before I tell my new husband who you are ".

"Well it's not that simple though is it, I have a child. I don't even know if I have a son or daughter. It's my right as a father to meet them ".

Linda felt dizzy. Sarah had never known who her father was, and Linda knew the right thing to do to would be to introduce them today and let her decide if she wanted to have a relationship with him. The foundations of her world were shaking, what she was about to do made her feel sick to her stomach.

"There was no baby, I had a miscarriage. I have no children, just nieces and nephews that I've always treated like my own. So if you'd stuck by me, who knows how it would have turned out. But you didn't. Don't ever come looking for me again."

She turned and walked away, her legs were shaking but she had never felt stronger, she went back to her guests, back to her husband, back to her future.

Mrs Brown's Sideboard

Rob Waites

English breakfast tea

Mr and Mrs Brown were married in 1946 after Mr Brown was demobbed from his service in the RAF. Given the housing shortage due to bombing they considered themselves very lucky to get a small flat on the top floor of a rather run-down house in London's East End.

Money was short and wartime restrictions meant that furnishings for their home were scrounged from friends and relatives or bought for a few shillings from second hand dealers. Much of this was "Utility" furniture produced to cope with war-time material shortages. Some of it was even older having served in the homes of a previous generation. Still, as Mrs Brown remarked, "It's not expensive items that make a happy home, it's love."

Over the succeeding years, things became easier with the post war boom creating rising standards of living. By the early 1960's, Mr and Mrs Brown were comfortable with Mr Brown having secured a job which came with accommodation.

The flat was new and although most of their existing furniture was an improvement on the old utility furniture they had as newlyweds, it had still been purchased second hand and was not as stylish and comfortable as the items Mrs Brown had seen in the windows of furniture shops. In particular their sideboard and dining table were still the original items purchased when they got married and had seen much better days! To move these into their new flat would be embarrassing and, as Mrs Brown had explained to Mr Brown, "On this new 'hire purchase scheme' you don't have to save up for things – you just put down a small deposit and then it's just a few bob a week. We'll hardly notice it and we can easily manage it out of your wages."

So, it was settled and after a few weeks, Mr and Mrs Brown were the proud possessors of a dining room suite comprising table, chairs and a sideboard containing a built -in cocktail cabinet. These were all in the latest "contemporary" style with the table and the sideboard finished in shiny laminate imitating mahogany, black legs splayed outwards in a cheeky avant-garde style and gold-coloured fittings. Mrs Brown invited friends in to see the latest additions and was suitably pleased by the admiring remarks. As she explained to her listeners grouped around the table, "You can even put a hot cup of tea on the tops and it doesn't mark them!"

The new furniture became her pride and joy, particularly the sideboard which was dusted and polished regularly. It also came to be used for displaying keep-sakes and small presents given to her by her children and, later, grandchildren.

In the late 1960s I got to know Mr and Mrs Brown through friendship with her son-in-law. When I visited their home the care she lavished on the sideboard was clear and it still looked as if it was on show in the furniture shop.

When I remarked on the sideboard my friend explained the history and I felt empathy with Mrs Brown. Not that I was a connoisseur of late 1950s' early 1960s' furniture. But I could understand how, someone brought up in the 1920s and 30s, probably surrounded by hand-me-downs from previous generations and who had started married life with war-time utility furniture, could feel a strong attachment bordering on love for the first new and comparatively expensive items of furniture in her life.

Sadly, after over 50 years of married life, Mr Brown died and Mrs Brown moved into a block of flats for elderly people. Downsizing possessions was necessary because of the size of the new accommodation but the prized sideboard was installed in a place of honour. It continued to be loved and polished regularly by Mrs Brown and the trinkets and keepsakes continued to grow in number. The drawers of the sideboard were filled with bits and pieces accumulated over the 40 plus years since it had been purchased.

All things pass and eventually so did Mrs Brown. As I was not a member of the family, I didn't hear about it at the time. However, I was contacted a couple of weeks later by her son-in-law. Mrs Brown's flat was owned by the local authority and it needed clearing promptly so that it could be prepared for the new tenant. I was asked to help as there were some heavy items to be shifted.

By the time I met up with my friend at the flat, his wife, and the few other relatives of Mrs Brown, had taken items which they wanted to remember her by leaving an assortment of odds and ends. A couple of charities were asked to take anything they could sell in their shops but when they came and the sideboard was pointed out to them, they all smiled and shook their heads. "There's no call for that old stuff now," was the reply.

We were left with some bundles of bits and pieces for the tip and… the sideboard!! What was to be done with it? We couldn't leave it in the flat as the Council would charge for removal. My friend had an idea. "There's a large bin store on the ground floor of the flats… we could take it down in the lift and put it in there."

I was a little dubious. Although the bin in the store was large, the sideboard would certainly stick out from the top. There would be no hiding it. However, no better idea occurred to us so we reverently carried the sideboard into the lift and took it down to the ground floor. We (still reverently) carried the sideboard outside and found the bin store door open. We hefted the sideboard up and over the side of the bin leaving it partially sticking out at the top!

As nonchalantly as we could we strolled away from the store trying to look as though this was a perfectly normal thing to put in the bin. I looked back from a safe distance and felt a twinge of guilt at seeing Mrs Brown's pride and joy dumped in a common or garden rubbish bin. I couldn't shake the idea that we had somehow discarded her life along with the sideboard. Silly I know but that is how I felt at the time – a feeling that hasn't diminished over the years.

About the author

Rob is 74 years old and has started writing fiction again after a gap of about 50 years. He was prompted to go on a creative writing course by his wife and this resurrected his interest in the genre.

Dear Ms Ginger Snaps

Erin McDougall

Peppermint latte

Holiday Blues got you down?

Does the Chipmunk's Christmas Medley on repeat make you want to deck your boss' halls? Tired of waiting under the mistletoe – you know it's a weed, right?

Write to Ms. Ginger Snaps with your tales of Christmas Woe!

She'll reply with sassy advice bound to brighten even the Scrooge-iest of Scrooges.

Give yourself the gift of Ms. Ginger Snaps!

Dear Ms. Ginger Snaps,

I need to face the facts: nobody likes me. I just don't get it. I'm everything anyone could possibly want: I'm sweet, I'm chewy and yeah, I can be a little nutty and sometimes a little dense, but if you nuke me for a few seconds, I'm soft and delicious too. But every year, at every party, I get stuck between Little Miss Perfect Shortbread and Brown Sugar Fudgey McFudgeface and I just don't stand a chance.

Sure, Miss Shortbread's all buttery and topped with a little fruity thing like those gaudy New Year's glasses people wear when they're elbow deep in the punch before 10PM, but everybody knows, she's super high-maintenance. What with all the mixing and chilling and making sure the butter is not too hard or too soft and blah blah blah. If I have to hear at one more party how she's the first one to get baked and how honoured she is to be the one to keep the holiday tradition going, I'll scream.

Then McFudgeface is all "aren't you the same Fruitcake from last Christmas, regifted back to the original gifter? Hahaha! Same cake, different plate, amiright?" I try to let it go but then I'm the last one standing at the end of the night and no one's picked me up, not even once out of courtesy for the host. Is there anything I can do to not get handed off as the oh-no-you-got-us-a-nice-bottle-of-wine-and-we-didn't-get-you-anything but-here's-a-Fruitcake-it's-homemade-Merry-Christmas-gift" this year? I'm even made with booze! Why am I so unlovable?

Sincerely,

Not Your Aunt Ruth's Fruitcake Again

Dear Not Your Aunt Ruth's Fruitcake Again,

I feel for you, Not Your Aunt Ruth's Fruitcake Again. The holiday party circuit is a tough nut to crack and this constant rejection and being the butt of terrible jokes has got to weigh on you. Take a deep breath of the pine-fresh air and relax. There is hope.

Your letter sparked a flood of messages:

"I love, love, LOVE fruitcake."

"I always look for the fruitcake at parties. Fruitcake is always interesting, complex and best when a little nutty."

"Keep your chin up! Fruitcake, like the little black dress, never goes out of style. And, like the little black dress, it takes a certain something to pull it off."

"My mother used to make fruitcake with those little candied red and green cherries. Mmm… go-od!"

So you see, Not Your Aunt Ruth's Fruitcake, you are appreciated. Loved! Compared to the one and only LBD. And if that doesn't give you a boost, then we're really in trouble.

Regarding Little Miss Shortbread and Brown Sugar Fudgey McFudgeface, what they say says more about them than it does about you. As a wise woman named Mrs Eleanor Roosevelt once said, "No one can make you feel inferior without your consent." It might also lift your spirits to know that Mrs Roosevelt's husband, The President, loved Fruitcake. So if you find yourself getting drawn into the drama with Shortbread and Fudgeface, feel free to bust out that ginger snap of a comeback.

Seriously, it's not you. It's them. By them, I mean society. Somewhere along the way of mass-food production, fruitcake got a rep for being a brick of spices and fruit that functions well as a doorstop and this is unfortunate. To be done justice, you're supposed to take days to make with only the best ingredients, spices and Scotch. You say you're "dense" and need a good "nuking" for your softness to really shine. I say, you deserve better. You are meant to be a thing of beauty, of moist, rich flavors that people ask about for the recipe. You deserve to be a creation of love and care and you need to demand this! No rushing, no regifting. Sugar Plum, you've gotta love yourself.

And know this, tastes cycle in and out like the latest gotta-have-it gift. I know you've been hurt before but you have to keep putting yourself, your BEST SELF out there. Your time will come. Soon enough, Little Miss Shortbread and Brown Sugar McFudgeface will be bragging about how they knew you way back when… and you'll be too busy making the party rounds to give these dark times any of your precious energy.

The Year of Aunt Ruth's Fruitcake looks both merry and bright!

Much Love,

Ms Ginger Snap

About the author

Calgary-based writer Erin McDougall loves the possibilities of the short story: writing contests, reviewing theatre and dance, plus snapshot bookstagram reviews on @thattowerofbooks. Her work has been published in *Toasted Cheese Literary Journal*, *The Culture Trip Paris*, and the anthology *WonderShift*.

Outwitted, Outplayed, Outdone Your Honour

Glen Donaldson

Dead Lawyer

The Right Honourable Chief Justice Lou Pohl could rock an intimidating stare with the best of them. It was an ability that had served him well over the course of a long and distinguished judicial career; one that had seen him come face to face with some of the country's most hardened felons.

Yet on the rare occasions mirth made an appearance in his courtroom, Judge Pohl was more than willing to sit back, along with everyone else, and enjoy the show. Today was one such occasion.

Newly-minted young lawyer Pickering Benedict was nervously attempting to cross-examine the State's senior most Coroner – a notoriously acid tongued, rotund gentleman known for not tolerating fools lightly nor sugar-coating anything not edible.

Under the microscope was the probable cause of death of two South Korean honeymooners killed during a thunderstorm. Improbably, the newlyweds had been 600 metres up in the air at the time, enjoying a hot-air balloon ride over Ayers Rock. Somehow and for some reason they'd both taken to gripping a metal-handled umbrella – "Mary Poppins" style – at the time. Yet the balloon operator was adamant no lightning strikes had taken place during the flight.

"Trial and error", with an emphasis on the latter, was the fresh-out-of-graduate-school lawyer's fumbling approach. Before it was all over, those present in the court would witness the perpetually stony-faced Judge wipe away tears of laughter.

PICKERING: Could you state your full name and date of birth for the court.

CORONER: Dr Arthur John Halliday, the 12th of August.

PICKERING: What year is that Mr Halliday?

CORONER: The 12th of August every year.

PICKERING: How many autopsies have you performed on dead people?

CORONER: They've all been on dead people sonny.

PICKERING: Do you recall approximately what time you examined the bodies?

CORONER: The autopsy commenced a little after 8pm the day of the incident.

PICKERING: Were the male and female dead at the time?

CORONER: If not they were by the time I finished with them.

PICKERING: Were you alone or by yourself when the autopsy was carried out?

CORONER: Think about what you just asked me, ace. My assistant Dr Peter Mannering was present also, if that's what you're getting at.

PICKERING: Doctor Halliday, prior to performing the autopsy on the first body, did you check for a pulse?

CORONER: No.

PICKERING: Did you check for blood pressure?

CORONER: No.

PICKERING: Did you check for breathing?

CORONER: No.

PICKERING: So then it is possible that the patient was alive when you began the autopsy?

CORONER: No.

PICKERING: How can you be so sure, Doctor?

CORONER: Because his brain was sitting on my desk in a jar.

PICKERING: I see, but could the patient have still been alive, nevertheless?

CORONER: Yes, it is possible that he could have been alive and practicing law.

PICKERING: No further questions your Honour. Thank you Dr Halliday for your insight, professionalism and measured responses.

CORONER: If I wasn't under oath squire, I'd return the compliment.

About the author

If Glen Donaldson were a wine he would be described as "light-bodied with a nutty aftertaste". He writes weekly at both *Scenic Writer's Shack* and *Lost In Space Fireside*.

DECEMBER

A Heart Called Petra *by Sarah Hills and* The Dance by Mary Daurio *have been chosen to wrap up a difficult year, ending 2021 with a glimmer of hope. December is one of the darkest months, but it is lifted by festivities with lights and celebrations of love. This is reflected in the two stories, both based around the heart. Two unique women, whose narratives end very differently, move through dense and difficult times, towards a sense of lightness as they each start to rekindle their life and spirit.*

About the editor

Linda Flynn has had books published for children and teenagers, as well as short stories for adults. Her anthology, *I Knew it in the Bath*, will be released in September 2022 with *Bridge House Publishing*. She can be found at: www.lindaflynn.com

The Dance

Mary Daurio

Root beer

Frightened by the West Nile Virus that's invading our little corner of Ontario, John's out shooting crows. How a mosquito could land on a crow to bite it is beyond me. I guess they do. He found a dead crow two days back. The damn thing was in the water trough. The coroner's report, death by drowning. Not West Nile.

There is no coroner, but yours truly. Still, he carries on. I wouldn't mind as much, but he's been drinking. Not soggy, he can load the gun, and he has one crow to his credit. It's just he is aiming in the direction of the chicken coop. If he hits my rooster or hens, it won't be West Nile he needs to fear.

I take him bug spray.

"Get that out of here. It's all chemical," John hollers.

Never mind, he's probably about eighty proof. That's an exaggeration, but still, he'll never notice the bites. Poetic justice, him getting bit by mosquitoes that may carry the West Nile. Or is that ironic? Whatever there is no talking to him while he's in this state. I go back inside to finish making supper.

Dusk settles, and in he stomps plunking the gun in the corner of the room.

"It's not loaded, is it?" I ask.

He raises his eyebrows in a bushing expression saying all he has to. It was those talking eyes that first drew me to him way back then in the heat of passion, before children and grandchildren, a lifetime ago. Sometimes even now, I look at him and get a pain in my side of love, and anguish.

"What's for supper?" John asks. Really, with the smell of corned beef in the air.

"I was afraid it might be rooster."

"Don't be ridiculous! I was miles from the coop."

That's not what I saw, but I keep my own counsel. Some things are easier let go, especially on a night like tonight. The local newspaper had a story about a crow testing positive for West Nile a few counties over from our farm. That's all it took to trip one of his dark moods. Best to just let it go. I decide to overlook the gun, in the corner and get the table ready for supper. Silence fills the air, that thick electric feeling just before a thunderstorm. It's been tipping tough these days with cattle prices down, and the seeding costing more – well, just about everything costing more.

"I have pie."

"That would be nice."

That's what we have between us. Once a roaring romance settles for polite passivity. Is this what happens to people who live together and share their lives? Does it all have to be eaten away?

Oh, John, what a dancer he was! People would

stare. We haven't been to a dance in twenty years. What would all those girls who wished they were me say if they could see us now? Anna Marie, especially. She would cut in on John and me back then. I'd smile and back away as he was going home with me, after all. To the best of my knowledge, he's been faithful. The farm, that's his other love, and I can't say I've not been jealous a time or two.

"I'm going with Joe to an auction tomorrow."

He brings me out of my reverie, and I startle a little at his voice.

"Don't need anything. Just want to see how the cattle and machinery go. Home for supper."

"Ask Joe in for the meal, if you like." Joe's farm is across the way. Widowed five years, and we have him over often. The men help each other back and forth when they have tough jobs to do.

"Yes, that would be a thought. Nice pie."

"Thanks," I say.

We ignore the tension between us and concentrate on the mundane little threads that twine us together. The safety net of the day to day that we often land in without any conscious thought.

He leaves the table and heads outside again to tinker with this machine or that. Haying season is just about here. He has a lot more to do than shoot crows. The gun stands a silent vigil in the corner. I'm not touching it, that's for damn sure. Stand on guard the rest of the week for all I care.

Instead of saying what is really bothering him, he sinks into the farm and all she needs. *What about me?* I want to scream. Is that selfish, or just self-preservation? I don't know, but somehow, I feel dwindled. Diminished, but not discarded. He spends more time maintaining his machinery than the time of day he gives me. I often wonder if he would notice if I served supper in the nude. I won't try it. What if he didn't notice?

He's up early today, and with the chores done, off with Joe. The day stretches ahead of me, and I have new energy. After every thunderstorm, the air clears and sparkles. It wasn't much of a storm between us last night, but enough to send me tossing and turning, finally going to sleep in the spare room. John says nothing about that this morning. Sad, but he is all business and auction. Where did your wife sleep last night, John? You who counts every cattle head. Well, at least I know where I stand. The air, while not exactly sparkling, is clear. We didn't have a thunderstorm, more like my own tumultuous sheet lightning.

I need to keep busy, so I make a couple more pies. Joe can take some home. I miss Joe's, Sarah. We had a friendship, close and consoling. I think of her when I offer Joe a meal or send him a pie.

Moulding all that dough, and flattening it with the rolling pin, is a type of therapy for me. With the children gone, John and I don't need much pie, so it's good to give some of that labour away. For the fowl supper at the church, I make ten pies. Just like that. Anyone who knows anything will say its sublimation. Oh, I read the kids' textbooks.

Things were different before they left for school and then started lives afterward. John is disappointed that none of the boys wanted to farm. When they were all home, life revolved around them and their needs. Ours went on the back burner. The same happens to a lot of folks. You lose your essence, the part that gives you your reason to be. John is finding his in the land and the farm he loves.

I can't compete.

He's got about two hundred acres. All five foot four of me, laid out flat, wouldn't be one-hundredth of an acre. Talk about a lightweight. I must be going crazy. He might be too.

I worried about him last winter when there was less to do, and he moped around, but spring has his engine running. He spends each waking hour working his fingers to the bone. He drinks on occasion, but nothing that has sent any alarms off yet, except for the crows.

The men return from the sale, and the meal is ready. The conversation is contained and stilted.

"Thanks, for a nice dinner, Alice," Joe says.

"How was the auction?" I ask.

"The cattle went cheap, and the machinery followed suit. Can't make anything farming, and can't make anything getting out. Eh, John?"

Up go John's eyebrows. He has been unusually quiet this evening. Oh, he answers questions, but he doesn't initiate anything. I wonder how he was at the sale with Joe. They have known each other most of their lives. Joe can usually get him out of the deep dark blue. No easy feat.

Joe takes his pie and thanks me.

I say, "We'll have to do this again soon, never mind waiting for an auction."

"That would be nice. Thanks again, Alice. Bye, John."

A silent wave from John, the screen door catches, and we are alone again. I thought he would come home in good humour from the sale. Joe is always pleasant company and even with things how they are farming, they commiserate and often share a joke.

I start to clear the dishes, and he leaves. My feet ache, so I throw my shoes off one at a time into the corner. I take another look, at the empty corner.

The gun is gone!

I hear a shot and a crunching noise.

Oh, Lord, no!

Running out, I see him aiming at the barnyard where all the cattle are milling around.

"John, stop! For God's sake, quit it."

He's ready to fire again but stops and turns to me like he's seen me for the first time.

His eyes look directly at me and his mouth grimaces. "Alice, what am I doing?"

"I'm not sure. Did you hit one?"

"No, I was aiming at the weather vane, the bullet hit the barn."

His hands tremble a little as he lays the gun on the grass. I take him in my arms. John holds me close and then takes a few steps. I realize we are dancing under the flickering illumination of the yard light, the moon and stars a canopy above us. The soft grass is a carpet beneath my bare feet, and those sweet tender steps of old send chills down my spine and bring tears to my eyes.

He holds me close and whispers in my ear.

"Alice, we need to go dancing more."

About the author

Mary Daurio is a grandmother who likes to fiddle with words, toot her flute, and spend time with family. She has had works published kindly by *CaféLit, The Fictional Cafe, Pure Slush Anthologies, Grey Borders, The Harrowsmith, Spillwords, Medium,* and *Friday Flash Fiction.*

A Heart Called Petra

Sarah Hills

First coffee of the day

How did I get here? How am I, Mrs Elizabeth Steadman, at this chilly lakeside, swimming costume in a plastic bag like a child at primary school, pretending I am here to get in the water? As if I would even put my feet into that soil-stained water? As if I am 9, not 59 years old, and I still have a heart called Petra.

When I was a small child, my heart became a kind of pet for me. I imagined this half wild, half-tamed fur creature burrowed into my chest, peeking out at the huge world. She was my invisible friend. I was Beth Morris in those days, and I called her Petra, after a dog on a children's TV show. I invited her to eat small snacks beside my plate at mealtimes, introduced her to people, placed a cushion beside my pillow at night for her. It was a phase that did not pass over as the usual phases of a young child. I grew older, adapted more to convention and no longer announced her to the dinner table. Nonetheless, Petra went everywhere with me.

The things I liked, Petra liked; spring and autumn, walking on clear days with the wind blowing in our faces, bird-watching, being by the sea, parties, presents, the summer sun when it lay like a sheen over everything. As I grew up, I liked to find new things to show Petra, to check out with her – do we enjoy this? Shall we do this? She loved dancing and people who made her laugh, reading books, making things.

I watch myself, a caricature of a middle-aged woman, grey-haired, practical cagoul, sensible shoes, large tummy and rounded back, shaking the hands of Duncan and Trish, both comfortingly substantial people. There is a group already swimming round pink and orange buoys bobbing in the black water. I am impossibly outside. The lake itself is implausible. I remember when this was a quarry and a slag heap, places to be avoided. Now, somehow, it is a wetland reserve and a lake to swim in. A future where I will get into that lake is a matter of science fiction.

"I've never swum outside." I begin. "In England, I mean. This isn't for me. It was the doctor's idea."

Trish smiles. "It's not deep on this side." Her plump hands shaking each other encouragingly across her stomach. "You don't have to swim at all. We have people who come just to walk up and down the far side, for the water resistance training."

She has misunderstood me. But before I can say anything further, Duncan, with the enthusiasm and exuberance of a puppy, despite his balding head and beer belly, is ushering me into a small prefab and showing me changing cubicles and piles of towels. There are rows of thermos flasks and trays of homemade brownies. For after.

"What have you got to lose?" Duncan says. He holds out a large orange towel. Petra liked orange.

The rough dry material scrapes against my palms releasing memories of swimming lessons as a child, swims with my own children, the feel-good sensation of getting dry after swimming. I let myself be bullied gently into changing.

Pulling on my swimming costume feels like dragging on one of those old diving suits. The ones with great round metal and glass bowls over the head. I cling to the towel round my shoulders and follow Trish out. More like a cow to the abattoir than a patient trying therapy.

The air alone is an affront to my bare skin. What am I doing? Where is the sticking place I can dig my heels in to and say, no way, not me? I count ten people doing laps on the circuit. The water is black, edged by reed beds full of sharp stalks. The sky is heavy with grey clouds.

"Now. It's best to wear these." Trish is holding up a pair of fabric slip-on shoes with rubbery soles. "So you don't slip, cos the bottom is mud, see?"

She is talking to me as if I am a child. She must be a primary school teacher. No. A dinner lady. Kindly, but no nonsense. You get what you are given.

I put on the slippers. Trish takes my hand, guides me forward till my toes are almost in the water. Duncan hovers to one side. He is wearing wet suit shorts and a huge T-shirt with "Wild swimmers do it in the Cold" printed across it.

When I met Robin Steadman, Petra loved him, with his wild mane of black hair and his serious politics. She loved his romance, his proposal. She was wild with joy when we married and moved in with him. Petra was there when our children were born. I became Mrs Elizabeth Steadman as Robin's career in IT took off and we entertained his clients and colleagues. Everyone called me Mrs Steadman, or Elizabeth. I was known as the wife who made that raspberry and cream pavlova.

Life got busy. Children. Work. Robin and I, we were good at life's administration. We were good at paying bills and making sure the kids got everything. We were good at making sure our house looked like it should, glossy and neat. It all worked like clockwork once we got the hang of it.

I do not know when I lost Petra. I remember thinking, one summer holiday in Greece, on a day so hot for once we could all only sit and be silent, that it must be OK; that Petra and I must have become one. I remember smiling to myself, because of course we had always been just one and it was crazy for me to keep thinking of my heart as a creature in her own right. A childish phase that I had somehow hung on to.

"Now, Elizabeth. Just take one step at a time." Trish could be encouraging a first day child into the playground. She has taken one of my hands and is looking at my feet intently. As if stepping off the shore is like stepping on to a thin, thin line and, if she is not careful, I might fall.

I am already falling. I think. I have been falling for years.

I take a step forward, up to my ankles.

The water is freezing. I gasp and something blasphemous is forced out between my lips.

Duncan grins. "Cold, isn't it?" He backs into the lake. "I find it best to take a few steps before you can think about it." He's up to his knees, shins showing white through the water, knees above bright red.

Trish frowns at him. "At your own speed, dear." She says to me. "There's no rush."

The swimming group come past us. I fear I will know someone, but they are all strangers. They call out to me. I can tell they think immersing one's whole body in ice is just one short step to happiness, jollity, even world peace.

I step after them and now I am knee deep. My feet hurt with the ice chill. My teeth chatter with the breeze coming across the lake.

"I can't do it."

Trish squeezes my hand. "You are doing so well. Really. It takes some people two goes to get to their knees."

"It's too cold."

Duncan flings out a fist in front of me, turns it up, opens his fingers and there is a jelly baby. "Sugar hit."

I look at him, but there's no hint of laughter here.

"Sugar hit." He repeats. "Helps to distracts you."

Someone calls out: "It took me a whole packet first time."

Duncan winks and brings out a packet he has been hiding behind his back. "I come prepared."

The next time I looked for her, Petra was dead. It was after the youngest child left home. There were evenings long as days and Robin was always at work. One day, sitting on the sofa watching re-runs of old films and eating chocolate, I realised the truth: Petra had died, and there was a dense, impacted weight in my chest.

Soon after that, it turned out that Robin was not at work after all. He and his new partner, Marielle – so bright, so adventurous, so French, so young – cut their ties (his ties) and bought backpacks, a flat in Paris. I kept the house. The children were pleased about that. It is good for holidays, for them.

I lost my part time job when I stopped turning up. That was six months ago. Recently, I realised that I had not left the house for a month; not spoken to a single person face to face.

I am not stupid, I can read the signs, so I went to the doctors. A busy, competent woman doctor diagnosed depression. Not surprising, she said, in the circumstances. She was kind but not sympathetic. The surgery was conducting a new trial, she explained, treating depression by activities rather than drugs. She showed me a list; group walking sessions at the local park; gym sessions at the sports centre; wild swimming. Then she hesitated and said that, unfortunately, only wild swimming was available.

I took the leaflet about it and went home. At first, the thought of water adding to the weight in my chest put me off. But then I realised water would not actually get into my chest and, obviously, there was not really a dead animal in place of my heart. I wondered if I should have told the doctor about Petra, if this would have counted as a delusion, and whether I would have been sectioned for my own safety. Then I wondered whether this thought was not just self-aggrandisement, and I was just over dramatising. A normal person would just get this all into perspective. I was stupid after all.

I have not had a jelly baby since the kids were kids. The sweet dissolves in my mouth as I take two more steps. I hold out my hand and Duncan places another sweet in my palm. Three sweets later, I am up to my middle.

Trish has let go my hand and is patting her shoulders with water. "It helps me prepare for the last bit."

I cannot do it. I gaze round: grey clouds layer above, while black water like liquid night stretches away to the reed beds. The peaty smell reminds me of rotting autumn leaves.

Someone calls out, "Heron!"

At the end of the lake, a grey sliver unfolds from another dimension huge wings and moves up into the sky. The bird crosses in front of me; a silent geometry of flight before swooping down beyond the reeds. Petra loved herons. I take a step towards it and another.

The mud disappears under my feet, I drop into the lake like the lump that I am. Freezing black wipes out all sensation: No breathing. No hearing. No seeing. I do not know which way is up. Fear and panic burst through me. I kick my legs out and meet nothing. I thrash my arms and feel the drag of the water.

In my chest, that deadweight rolls over. Petra gets to her feet, shakes herself in the cold biting blackness. I stop struggling, suspended in the darkness, my heart is thudding, great drumming beats. Petra looks up, I look up and the water is lighter above me.

Three strokes bring me to the surface. Hands grab mine and Duncan's bulk heaves me back onto mud. I can hear myself spluttering. I can hear Trish apologising.

"You can go straight in and dry off." Trish is saying. "That's quite alright."

"Now let's hold on." says Duncan. "Let Elizabeth get her breath."

I'm colder above the water than below. I bend my knees to get my shoulders back under, push my wet hair back out of my eyes, Petra still moving about in my chest, making room for herself.

"Beth." I say. "Call me Beth."

I look at the expanse of the lake rippling under the open sky with the wind passing over it, the trees at the far end coming into the fresh green of spring. "I think I'd be OK to swim a bit." I say.

About the author

Sarah lives in the North of England and has recently started taking her writing seriously.

Index of Drinks

Like to Read More Work Like This?

Then sign up to our mailing list and download our free collection of short stories, *Magnetism.* Sign up now to receive this free e-book and also to find out about all of our new publications and offers.

Sign up here:
http://eepurl.com/gbpdVz

Please Leave a Review

Reviews are so important to writers. Please take the time to review this book. A couple of lines is fine.

Reviews help the book to become more visible to buyers. Retailers will promote books with multiple reviews.

This in turn helps us to sell more books… And then we can afford to publish more books like this one.

Leaving a review is very easy.

Go to https://bit.ly/3IIgRm3, scroll down the left-hand side of the Amazon page and click on the "Write a customer review" button.

Writing for CaféLit

Have you got a story in you? Do you think it would suit CaféLit?

We're looking for thought-provoking and entertaining stories, though ones which might be a tad different from what you normally read in a woman's magazine. They should be the sort of length that would make easy reading whilst you drink a cup of coffee, even if you linger a while, but without you needing to rent a table.

So, perhaps, no more than 3000 words. Shorter stories and flash fiction are naturally very welcome.

We'll read your story. If we like it, we'll let you know and if we don't like it we'll let you know – within a month. We will work on editing with you.

Each year we'll publish a volume of the best stories. If you are in the volume you will have a share of the profits.

Our editing process will also include some work on your bio to maximise its effect.

We also ask you assign your story the name of a drink. Something light and frothy might be a hot chocolate. A dark piece of flash fiction could be an espresso. Something good for the soul would be a mint tea.

Full submission details can be found at www.cafelit.co.uk/index.php/submission-guidelines-2.

Also by Chapeltown Books

“The Best of CaféLit” series

Each story in these little volumes is the right length and quality for enjoying as you sip the assigned drink in your favourite Creative Café.

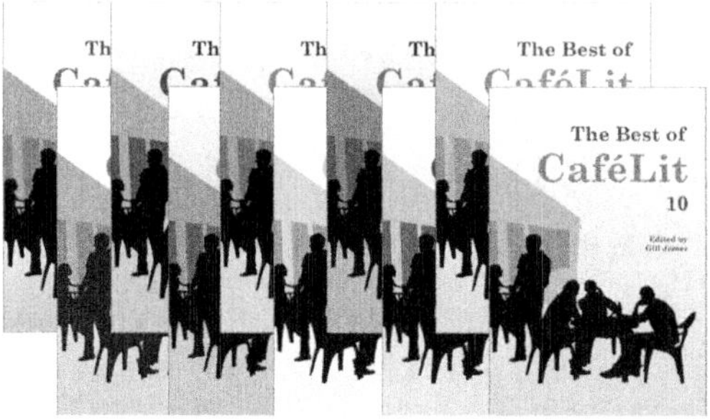

Order from Amazon:

CaféLit 2011
ISBN: 978-0-9568680-3-9 (paperback) 978-0-9568680-4-6 (ebook)
CaféLit 2012
ISBN: 978-0-9568680-8-4 (paperback) 978-0-9568680-9-1 (ebook)
CaféLit 3
ISBN: 978-1-910542-00-2 (paperback) 978-1-910542-01-9 (ebook)
CaféLit 4
ISBN: 978-1-910542-02-6 (paperback) 978-1-910542-03-3 (ebook)
CaféLit 5
ISBN: 978-1-910542-04-0 (paperback) 978-1-910542-05-7 (ebook)
CaféLit 6
ISBN: 978-1-910542-17-0 (paperback) 978-1-910542-18-7 (ebook)
CaféLit 7
ISBN: 978-1-910542-40-8 (paperback) 978-1-910542-41-5 (ebook)
CaféLit 8
ISBN: 978-1-910542-45-3 (paperback) 978-1-910542-46-0 (ebook)
CaféLit 9
ISBN: 978-1-910542-54-5 (paperback) 978-1-910542-55-2 (ebook)
CaféLit 10
ISBN: 978-1-910542-76-7 (paperback) 978-1-910542-77-4 (ebook)

Chapeltown Books

The Jinn

by Mason Bushell

At just five-inches tall, he's a demon with attitude, and he is fed-up with people summoning him through his talisman. With sass and cheek aplenty, he wanders grumpily through a saga of adventures. He meets learner drivers, babies, and zoo creatures, to name but a few, each in need of his special brand of help.

"Mason Bushell has created an amusing little character in the Jinn & you can't help but smile at his antics & the way he expresses himself. If you are looking for a quick fast read that will leave you with a smile, give it a read." (*Amazon*)

Order from Amazon:

Paperback: ISBN 978-1-910542-62-0
eBook: ISBN 978-1-910542-63-7

The Basilwade Chronicles

by Dawn Knox

The Basilwade stories were originally published on the CaféLit website, where you can access short stories that go nicely with a cuppa. We even suggest a drink! Dawn Knox's stories contain characters and situations that may seem a little larger than life at first glance but we can soon see that everyone involved is very human. And don't we all recognise the quirkiness of village/small-town life?.

"It's been a long time since I spent so much of my time laughing while reading a book. Endlessly inventive, crackling jokes, no two characters alike. And every story ends, not with a cliffhanger or a hook into the next one, but the eager need to answer the question, 'NOW WHAT HAPPENS?'

"If Basilwade doesn't actually exist somewhere, it thoroughly deserves to!" (*Amazon*)

Order from Amazon:

Paperback: ISBN 978-1-910542-49-1
eBook: ISBN 978-1-910542-47-7

Chapeltown Books

The Macaroon Chronicles

by Dawn Knox

The Macaroon Chronicles is a romp through relationships amongst some anthropomorphic characters. It is one of those quirky books that awakes your sense of humour. Come and follow the fun.Take a tour of the exotic Isle of Macaroon with Eddie and his zany friends who will be pleased to show you the cheese mines, Meringue Mountains and the Custard River while they flee unscrupulous promoters, bandit badgers and low-flying seagulls.

"This book is a joyous romp through absurdity, where the characters are all animals, the scenery is mostly edible and the events propel the action at breakneck speed. It's not Animal Farm, but a more gentle look at the everyday emotions of a group of friends battling their way through life. Not to be missed." (*Amazon*)

Order from Amazon:

Paperback: ISBN 978-1-910542-60-6
eBook: ISBN 978-1-910542-61-3

Dramatic Episodes

by Janet Howson

These interlocking episodes give us an insight into the complexities of 21st Century life. They are interconnected through the activities of an amateur dramatic group. Here we see the drama of real life unfold.

"This book is a must-read for anyone who is involved in Am Dram or who knows anything about it. Cleverly written individual stories which make up a larger story about an amateur dramatic performance. Written in a very chatty style, as if a friend is recounting stories to you! Great read!" (*Amazon*)

Order from Amazon:

Paperback: ISBN 978-1-910542-70-5
eBook: ISBN 978-1-910542-71-2